THE DARK LEGACY

SHEFFIELD MURDERS FROM PAST TO PRESENT

J.R. Hensby

THE DARK LEGACY

SHEFFIELD MURDERS FROM PAST TO PRESENT

First published 2025
J.R. Hensby

Acknowledgements

A big thank you to my friends Barbara Lucas, Carol Massey and Shirley Parent for proof reading and for their support and encouragement.

CONTENTS

INTRODUCTION

Sheffield. City of Steel. The fifth largest city in England; it is built on seven hills, with some areas of outstanding natural beauty and some iconic landmarks.

It has a vibrant community, but like cities everywhere the city harbours a darker, more sinister legacy: a legacy of chilling crimes.

This book delves into these unsettling stories. From the foggy streets of the Victorian era to the vibrant city of today you'll find details of murders that have left an indelible mark on Sheffield's collective memory.

Each chapter offers an insight into the motives, methods and consequences of these terrible crimes.

Read on and uncover the dark truths that lie hidden within the history of this remarkable city.

CHAPTER ONE: William Smedley. The last Sheffield man to be hanged

The second world war created devastation in the north of England, but the bombed ruins of houses and buildings provided a good playground for children. I well remember that as a child in the 1950's my friends and I played on a site just over the wall from our house where two houses had been bombed and almost demolished. The walls that remained were perfect for us to sit inside and play, sheltered if necessary from the cold wind.

The winter of 1947 was extremely cold with frequent heavy falls of snow but on Saturday morning the 8th of March eleven year old Peter Johnson was out and about in the bomb damaged buildings as usual. Clambering through an outbuilding on Spring Street near to the City Centre of Sheffield he was shocked to find the dead body of a woman with a scarf tied tightly around her neck. Losing no time he sped to his home at the Stag Inn on Wilson Street and gasped out to his father, the licensee of the pub, the story of what he had found.

 The police were immediately informed and they had no difficulty in identifying the dead woman because she was a prostitute who plied her trade in the local public houses and was well known to the police. Her name was Edith Simmonite and she was 27 years old. For the past six or seven years she had lived in a hostel on West Bar Green.

The police began their enquiries by visiting the hostel to see what they could learn there. The landlord, Charles Fisher, told them that Edith had gone out as usual on Friday the 7th of March and he had not seen her since.

Next they visited the local public houses that Edith was known to frequent and at a pub called The Sun Inn a barmaid called Winnie Bentley said that Edith had been in the pub on Friday the 7th of March and that she had been drinking with two men: William Smedley and Matthew Frayne and the police went and interviewed these two men. Smedley told them that he had left Edith at the steps to the hostel, but when Frayne was interviewed he said that when he went into the hostel Smedley was still talking to Edith. Charlotte Johnson who made up the beds in the hostel said that Smedley's bed had not been slept in on the 7th of March and the man who occupied the bed next to him confirmed what Charlotte had said.

Police enquiries weren't getting very far however and after six weeks it was obvious that the case was going cold, but it was just about to heat up:

On the 9th of May Smedley sent a telegram to his sister Dora Butler. It read: "Come Saturday morning. Urgent. Brother in trouble".

Doris did as requested and he confessed to her that he had committed the crime.

We don't know what advice she gave to him but on the afternoon of that same day he went to the police station in Doncaster and spoke to Detective Sergeant Naylor. He told him that shortly after the murder a man that he knew had confessed to him that he had murdered Edith and that he was leaving Sheffield and going to live in Rhyl, North Wales, to avoid being suspected and interviewed by the police. Smedley said that he didn't know the man's name but that he was a long-haired Irishman. He had now received a letter from the man asking him to come to Rhyl for a meeting the following Monday. He did not know why the man would want to meet him and he was unable to produce a copy of the letter. DS Naylor said that he would travel to Rhyl with him on Monday and they would both meet the Irishman. The Irishman failed to turn up but the detective and Smedley stayed in the area; asking around as to whether anyone knew of a long haired Irishman who had arrived in town recently. Their efforts to find the man failed and for reasons known only to himself Smedley suddenly decided to confess to the murder. He was cautioned and then made the following statement:

"I went out of The Sun Inn with Edith at 10 pm on Friday the 7th of March and stood talking to her at the bottom of the steps to her hostel. She was nagging at me. I went down Spring Street about 10.15 pm. I went into an old building on Bridge Street. I then got hold of her scarf and pulled it tight but I didn't mean killing her. She had the scarf around her neck and I pulled it tight in a single knot. I took the scarf around the top of her head but I can't remember whether I tied the ends or not. Suddenly she dropped back and stopped struggling. I got back to the hostel around 11.20 pm. The reason I did it was that she had given me a disease and was always taunting me. My intention was to frighten her so she would keep away from me. I was getting fed up. I had a letter from an Irishman last Wednesday to go and meet him at Rhyl outside the Yorkshire Miners Convalescent Home. This man was at the hostel on the 9th of March 1947 and I told him I had killed Edith. I also told Matthew Frayne the same day. What I've written is the truth. I am not pleading guilty to murder but I am admitting that it was me that killed her."

Smedley was tried at Leeds before Mr. Justice Pritchard on the 21st and 22nd of July 1947. He did not have a defence counsel and defended himself. He told the court that he had had no intention of hurting the girl and argued that this was manslaughter and not murder. The jury did not agree with him and he was found guilty of murder and sentenced to death by hanging. He did not mount an appeal but there was some controversy surrounding the trial in relation to the evidence, the motive, and the verdict, and these issues were raised by the media and the public.

In relation to the evidence, some people questioned the reliability of Smedley's confession which was made after a long and exhausting journey to Rhyl with a police officer. They wondered whether he had been coerced or influenced by the detective to admit to the crime. They also pointed out that there was no forensic evidence linking him to the murder scene, such as fingerprints, or bloodstains matching his blood group. Some people argued that he had no clear motive to kill Edith, who he had known for some months and with whom he had been drinking on the night of the murder. They pointed out that he was a hard-working miner who had been driven to desperation by the woman's taunts about giving him a venereal disease. They said that he was not a habitual criminal and that he was merely a victim of his circumstances. There was disagreement from some people in relation to the jury's decision to find him guilty of murder rather than manslaughter. They believed that he had acted in a moment of passion and had no intention of hurting the girl. The Sheffield Star newspaper printed a letter from a reader who wrote "I think it is a shame that a man should be hanged for a crime committed in a moment of passion. He was not a habitual criminal, but a hard-working miner who had been driven to desperation by the woman's taunts. Surely there is enough mercy in this world to spare such a man from the gallows". Many other people also considered the death penalty itself to be barbaric. The Leeds Mercury published an editorial that argued: "The execution of William Smedley is a grim reminder of the futility and cruelty of the death penalty. It does not deter crime, it does not reform the criminal, it does not satisfy justice, it does not console the victim's relatives. It only adds another tragedy to the one already committed. It is time for this country to abolish this relic of barbarism and join the ranks of civilised nations that have done away with it." In view of these concerns the Home Secretary was petitioned to show mercy and clemency for Smedley but pleas were ignored, and he was hanged at Armley prison, Leeds, by Steve Wade and Harry Kirk on Thursday the 14th of August 1947. He was the last Sheffield man to be hanged; but he wasn't the only Sheffield man called William Smedley to have had a date with the hangman.

Photo of of Edith Simmonite who was murdered by William

Smedley in 1947

CHAPTER TWO: 1875. Another Sheffield murderer called William Smedley

William Smedley was born in 1825 in Sheffield, the son of a cutler. He worked as a knife-maker and grinder, but he was also involved in trade unionism and radical politics. He was a member of the Sheffield Trades Council and the Sheffield Reform League. He supported the Chartists and the International Working men's Association. He was also a vocal opponent of the Crimean War and the American Civil War, so we can assume that he was a man of some intelligence and also of some standing in the local community. He had married Mary Ann Smith in 1847 and they had six children together. It seems a fairly reasonable assumption that by 19th century working class standards William Smedley's life was fairly good.

Obviously not good enough for him however because in 1870, like many a man before him and since, 45 year old William started an affair with a younger woman. Her name was Elizabeth Frith and she was fifteen years younger than him. She was born in Huddersfield in 1840; the daughter of a woollen spinner, and she had married a man called John Frith in 1861. He was a tailor and they had four children together. The couple and their children moved to Sheffield in 1869 and she became a dressmaker - probably linked to her husband's job as a tailor. Her affair with William Smedley began a year after their move to Sheffield.

She left her husband in 1874, and William left his wife and they moved into a new home together. I suppose they expected that this would be the beginning of a happy new life together but things soon started to go wrong. In 1875, at the age of fifty, William's eyesight started to deteriorate, and his employer sacked him from his job as a knife maker. With no welfare state this plunged the family into poverty and Elizabeth soon grew tired of this hand-to-mouth existence and she ended their relationship. She moved into another house without telling him where she was going and refused to see him again.

William wouldn't accept that the relationship was over and managed to find out her new address at a flat on Rockingham Street. At about 8.30 pm on Tuesday August the 31st he went to the house and knocked on the door. She opened the window and told him to go away. He begged her to let him in but she refused. He took a razor out of his pocket and said "If you don't let me in I'll slit your throat". She laughed at him and said "You can't do it". He then climbed up the wall and reached the window. Grabbing her by the hair, he slit her throat with the razor; almost decapitating her. He then jumped down and ran away, leaving her bleeding to death.

To his credit, William did not try to escape or hide his crime. He went to a nearby pub and asked for a glass of water. He told the landlord that he had just killed his wife and showed him his bloody hands and the razor. He then walked to the police station and surrendered himself. He confessed everything to the police and said that he loved Elizabeth more than anything in the world, but he could not bear to lose her. He also said that he was sorry for what he had done and hoped that God would forgive him.

His trial took place on Monday the 29th of November 1875 at Leeds Assizes before Mr Justice Mellor. William pleaded Guilty, but his counsel argued that he was insane at the time of the crime. They presented evidence that there was a history of mental illness within his family, his political agitation, his alcoholism, his jealousy and his remorse. They also called several witnesses who testified that he was a kind and honest man who had been driven mad by love.

The prosecution was having none of that however. They argued that he was sane and responsible for his actions. They pointed out that he had planned the murder beforehand and that he had shown no signs of insanity before or after the crime. They contended that he had acted out of revenge and anger rather than love. They also called several witnesses who testified that Elizabeth was a respectable woman who had been treated cruelly by William. The jury deliberated for only an hour before returning their verdict of Guilty, and the judge sentenced him to death by hanging.

His execution took place at Armley Prison a month later on Tuesday the 21st of December 1875 at 8 a.m. He was calm and composed on the scaffold and made no statement or confession before his death. He was hanged by Thomas Askern, the official executioner for Yorkshire, and his body is buried within the prison grounds.

CHAPTER THREE: Charles Hall, a Sheffield man sentenced to hang in 1953

As we saw in the first chapter of this book, William Smedley was the last Sheffield man to be hanged. Not a "claim to fame" he would have wanted of course, and he almost didn't get it because another Sheffield man was tried for murder in 1953 and sentenced to hang. The trail of events leading to this judgement was very tragic: a devoted father driven by despair to murder his son. It was Thursday the 15th of October1953 and a woman called Olive Mayhew who lived at No 7 Longley Crescent was worried. She hadn't seen her next door neighbour Charles Hall or his disabled son John since the previous afternoon. Nowadays it is, sadly, not terribly unusual to read about cases where people have lain dead in their home for days, weeks, or even years without anyone becoming concerned enough to check whether anything is amiss. But this was the 1950's and this was working class Sheffield. There was a proper sense of community, which still exists today in many parts of Sheffield, and people looked out for their neighbours, and it was completely out of the ordinary for Mrs Mayhew not to have seen Charles or John since the day before. 65 year old Charles Hall was retired from work and like many Sheffield men before him and since he had spent his working life as a steelworker; a steel smelter to be precise, in the great "City of Steel". His son John was 24 years old and severely disabled. His mental age was only about three to seven years old and he needed constant care and attention. Until his wife Jessie's death from cancer in 1950 at the age of 60, she and Charles had spent 24 years caring devotedly for their son and after her death Charles continued to care for John with the same love and attention. But the strain of this was beginning to tell on him. He was now 65 years old and the average life expectancy of a man who had done manual work in the steelworks was only 67 years, and Charles was worrying about what would become of his son when he could no longer look after him. These worries played so much on his mind that he was convinced that he himself was suffering from cancer. Hospital tests had ruled this out but Charles remained unconvinced and he was tormented with fear about what would happen to his son after he was no longer there to care for him. John was unable to speak or attend to his own personal care and nor could he do any of the necessary tasks of daily living

Mrs Mayhew was no doubt aware of Charles' worries and how they were having a very negative impact on his own health so she thought she had better go round and check that all was well. She knocked at their door and when she got no reply she asked a neighbour - one of the few to have a phone in the house in those days - to call the police. The police were soon on the scene and when they couldn't get any response from inside the Hall's property, they smashed the glass in the front door and broke in. They found Charles and John lying unconscious in the front room and the room was filled with the smell of coal gas. Unfortunately, John was not unconscious but dead. Charles was unconscious but in a critical condition and he was rushed to the City General Hospital on Herries Road. It seemed to be a very tragic accident caused by a leak of gas from the gas fire in the room. A hint that all was not as it seemed at first glance could be seen by the fact that a police officer sat by Charles' bed waiting for him to regain consciousness. Meanwhile on December 22nd, a week after his death, John was laid to rest in the same grave as his devoted mother Jessie (née Antcliffe) in the City Road Cemetery.

When he regained consciousness Charles immediately confessed that he had killed John. He told the police officer at his bedside that he had been living in despair and could no longer cope. All he could see was his own slow painful death from cancer, leaving his son without anyone to care for him. The only solution to this heartbreaking situation was, in his mind, that they should both die together and he turned on the gas fire in the living room without lighting it, in the belief that the poisonous gas would kill them both. As we know, it did kill John but Charles had been lying next to the gas fire and it seems that a down draft of air coming down the chimney provided him with enough oxygen to stay alive. He was arrested, discharged from hospital and taken into custody.

His trial began at Leeds Assizes on Monday the 23rd of November 1953 before Mr Justice Sable. Charles stood in the dock, wearing a hearing aid and pleaded Guilty to the murder of his son. One would expect in all circumstances that a person accused of murder would accept the advice of his defence counsel to mount a defence against the charge and require the prosecution to find him guilty "beyond all reasonable doubt" but Charles would not allow the defence to do that. They could probably have mounted a reasonable defence of diminished responsibility but again Charles did not want them to do that.

I think that it's easy for any person of compassion to understand the reasons why Charles might do this. His intention was for him to die alongside his son yet he had survived and he must have considered himself truly "guilty". Maybe he even thought that the hangman would finish the job that he had started and in killing him complete the plan and reunite him, in death, with his beloved son.

The judge was understandably perturbed about this unusual situation and he asked Charles' defence counsel Mr J.F. Drabble Q.C whether he had fully explained the implications of this course of action to the defendant. Mr Drabble replied that Hall had fully understood the consequences, and that the course that Hall had taken had caused extreme anxiety to those who advised him. Mr Drabble explained the background to the case: how John had been severely disabled from birth and that he had received devoted care from his parents for the 24 years that he lived. He said that Hall, convinced that he himself had cancer and fearing what would become of his son, had decided that the only solution to this terrible situation was that they should both die together.

In 1953 the only sentence that a judge was allowed to give for murder was the death penalty. It's easy to understand why Charles' defence counsel and the judge were both very concerned about his decision to only allow the truth of what happened to be told without any mitigating circumstances of any kind. The judge turned to the prosecutor, Mr J Basil Herbert QC, and said "On the information available to the Crown, do you know of any reason why I should not accept the plea of Guilty?" Mr Herbert replied "Not that I know of".

One can feel the judge's unease about the situation because he then asked Mr Drabble whether Charles was fully rational and fully aware of the course he had taken and Mr Drabble replied "He seems to be so", and that was it. Under the law the judge had no choice and he donned the black cap and the sentence of death was given. Charles was led out of the courtroom to await his fate. The whole trial had lasted barely five minutes. The date of his execution was provisionally fixed for the 15th of December, exactly two months after the death of his son.

The people of Sheffield were horrified about what was happening and quickly sprang into action to prevent what they saw as a grave miscarriage of justice. The Revd. Howard Hall (no relation to Charles), the vicar of the local St Leonard's church, and his congregation set about organising a petition to ask the Home Secretary for clemency. Before long they had collected more than 3,000 signatures. Revd. Hall wrote to the Home Secretary to advise him of the very strong public opinion against the execution of Charles Hall and that more than 3,000 people had already signed a petition. A further 1,300 workers at a major steelworks also signed a petition which was quickly sent off to the Home Secretary.

At 3.30 a.m on the morning of the 1st of December 1953 Charles was woken up by a prison warder to say that they had been informed that he had been reprieved and was no longer under sentence of death. The next person to hear the news was his next door neighbour Olive Mayhew. A telegram sent from the prison read "Reprieve through. Thanks. Charles".

One can easily imagine the great relief and happiness when the news quickly spread. George Tomkins, his next door neighbour at number 3, told the local press "He did everything for his son. We thought a lot of him. He is a good, kind God-fearing man and we hope he'll be home before long". Mr Vincent Hughes, the City Council's housing manager, said that Charles' house would be kept open for him. His kindly neighbour Olive Mayhew looked after the house, keeping it warm, clean and habitable ready for the day when he would come home.

When would that day be though? One would reasonably expect that a death sentence that had been reprieved would be replaced by a life term in prison but that's not what happened to Charles. He was released within a year, back to live at no 5. Longley Crescent amongst the people who had helped and supported him.

An online Social group called Sheffield History and Expats discussed the case in 2012 and it provides some interesting information about the case. A member of the group called Ceegee posted a link to an article in The Times newspaper dated the 24th of November 1954: "Charles Hall, aged 66, steel smelter of Longley Crescent, Sheffield has been released from prison. Nearly a year ago he was reprieved after being sentenced to death for the murder of his imbecile son."

Another member called Hillsbro posted that marriage records show that Charles remarried in 1957. His wife was called Elizabeth Stuart and they lived together at 5 Longley Crescent until Charles died in 1963 at the age of 74.

A post on the site from Penfold 2005 fascinates me as I have a strong interest in the supernatural.

He wrote: "I lived at that house in question for 30 yrs from 1970 and must say a very happy and loving home. My mom never knew that there was a murder at the property but my father did and never said anything to my mother or us as we would have never moved there, Mr Hall was pardoned for the murder with support from the clergy who was at St' Leonards Church at the time and its parishioners and the community who submitted over a 3,000 signed petition, The murder took place in the large front room on the front of the house and Mr Hall was found near to the old fireplace where he passed out, he survived because he was getting air from the chimney flue.

As a boy who lived in the house I and my family feel that the presence of Mr Hall still remains there in spirit as there was some strange things that went off in that bedroom e.g. feeling of hand pushing down on your face whilst sleeping, checking that you're OK when no one is there, shadows of figures standing there at the side of the bed, also hearing slight movement in the room when there is no one there may be his son or Mr Hall himself."

A big thank you to all those contributors who provided such valuable and interesting information. I do hope that Charles and his son John are resting in peace.

The house on Longley Hall Crescent where Charles Hall
murdered his son John in 1953

CHAPTER FOUR: 1884. The Tragedy of the Laycock family

Thankfully, Charles Hall was treated with understanding kindness and compassion but unfortunately Joseph Laycock wasn't so lucky.

In 1884, 35 year old Joseph was living at no 2 White Croft with his 25 year old wife Maria and their four children; 8 year old Sarah, 6 year old Mary, 4 year old Frank and 2 year old Joseph. Maria was in the late stages of pregnancy with her fifth child. White Croft is a group of houses which were not far from the City Centre; it was in a highly industrialised area and the properties, which were occupied by working class families, were often overcrowded and insanitary.

Joseph worked as a hawker, but he was absent from work more often than he turned up, mainly because he had a serious drink problem. In May of 1884, Joseph had been called up for military training but by July of that year he was back home and soon in trouble with the police for assaulting his wife Maria for which he received a 21 day prison sentence. I don't know a lot about the military but I would guess that it was not usual for a man to serve for less than a couple of months. In view of later events, and medical evidence given at his later trial, I would hazard a guess that he had been deemed unsuitable for the military due to mental health problems and discharged.

He arrived home after serving his 21 day sentence on
Saturday the 5th of July but it would appear that serving
time for assaulting his wife hadn't made him think twice
about doing it again because he was overheard threatening to
"do her in" on that same evening and It was only five days
later on Thursday the 10th of July that he carried out his
threat. The couple had gone out drinking that evening and
seemed to be on quite friendly terms. They left for home at
about 11 pm but about an hour later dreadful screams were
heard, although the person who heard them didn't know
where they were coming from.

The Times newspaper gave one of the first reports on the
murders on the 12th of July. They reported the dreadful
scene that was discovered at the house on the morning of the
11th of July. When there was no sign of either Joseph, Maria
or their four children by 10 o'clock that morning neighbours
became concerned. Working class areas in Sheffield in the
19th century (and even in the 20th) had a wonderful
community spirit and neighbours looked out for each other
and helped each other as needed. In usual circumstances I
would expect that one of the neighbours would pop round to
check on things but maybe because of the screams that had
been heard the previous night and also knowing of Joseph's
habit of assaulting Maria they decided that it would be safer
to go to investigate what was happening as a group. Three
women went to the house. When no-one answered their
knock they opened the door, calling for Maria as they
walked in. They discovered the most dreadful scene. Maria
was lying on her back in a pool of blood with her throat cut.
One of the women went upstairs to see whether the children
were alright but just inside the bedroom door she found
Joseph lying in a pool of blood. She thought that he too was
dead but one of his legs moved and knowing how violent he
could be she ran back downstairs to the other two women.

The three women had no idea where the children were but they hurried to the nearby police station and gasped out the terrible story of what they had found.

Sergeant Hornsey was soon at the scene and went upstairs to see what the situation was. He found Joseph lying on the floor with his throat gashed. He knew the police officer and said "Bob. Let me die. Don't move me. Let me die". The officer looked round the room and saw all four of the children lying on the floor with their throats cut. Their bodies were cold so they had obviously been dead for a considerable time. Sgt. Hornsey didn't let Joseph die; he arranged for him to be quickly transferred to the Sheffield Public Hospital on West Street. His injuries turned out not to be life threatening and he confessed to the murders the following afternoon.

He made the statement to one of the surgeons at the hospital. He said that he understood the fate that awaited him – that he would be hanged for the murders. He said that he and his wife had come home from the pub that night and that they were both drunk. His wife told him that she wished that she was dead and he lost his temper and cut her throat with a bread knife from the kitchen and she died quickly. He had then gone upstairs and cut the throats of his three oldest children. Then he took his youngest; two year old Joseph on his knee and cuddled him. The child said to him "Don't do it to me dada" but Joseph took the knife and slit the youngster's throat before then using the knife on himself and cutting his own throat. The thought of that poor young boy being cuddled by his daddy and asking his daddy not to kill him is heartbreaking beyond words. As he stayed in hospital recovering, Maria and her four children were laid to rest in one grave at the Intake cemetery. Thousands of people, horrified by the tragedy, gathered nearby and many police were needed to keep control of such a large number of people although everyone paid their respects peacefully. The inquest into the deaths took place on the 25th of July. Joseph was still in hospital and not well enough to attend. Although earlier reports had said that Joseph and Marie were on friendly terms in the pub the night before the murders, evidence at the inquest sheds some doubt on that. The barman said that on that night the couple had had something to eat together, and Joseph tried to order a drink for Maria and himself. She said that she didn't want a drink. He had replied "You might as well get drunk tonight while you have the chance". She said once again that she didn't want a drink and he had said that it might be the last chance she ever got to have any drink. No doubt fearing another beating Maria had had little choice but to comply with his demand and have a drink. One Of the neighbours who had found the bodies and the injured Joseph the next morning gave evidence of what she had seen and about the police being sent for. She said that the knife used to commit the murders was lying beside Joseph so, unsurprisingly, the jury found him guilty of wilful murder and he awaited his trial whilst still in hospital.

The trial began on the 5th of August, less than a month after the murders. As is usual in multiple murders he was tried for only one of them; that of his oldest child, eight year old Sarah. Obviously Joseph had committed a terrible crime, but it does not fit well with me that he would be hauled into court to face justice when he was still in the early stages of recovering from his failed suicide attempt and the resulting serious injury that he had inflicted on himself. He had to be carried prostrate into the courtroom and provided with a chair in the dock because he was incapable of standing. He was desperately upset and cried bitterly; with his head down and resting on the rail of the dock throughout the proceedings. Details of the court proceedings were given in

The Times newspaper on the 6th of August: It began with the prosecutor, Mr C. M. Atkinson, outlining the details of the crime. He said that on the afternoon of 10th July, the prisoner had stopped a police constable in the street and told him that his wife Maria had been drinking with another man. He was apparently sober when he said this. He had returned home to his wife and children at about six o'clock and he and his wife then went out together to a local public house for supper. He had said to his wife that she may as well get drunk while she had the chance. His wife had replied that she did not want any drink and he had said to her that it might be the last time that she would get any. They left the public house at about 10 pm and were heard quarrelling in the street. At about eleven o'clock a neighbour called Mrs Kidnew heard the shutters of the Laycock house being closed and a short while later the woman had heard screams but she did not know where the screams came from. She was passing the house the next morning at about eight or nine o'clock and noticed that the shutters were still closed, which was unusual, so she had opened the door and gone inside and seen the body of the prisoner's wife lying on the floor with her throat cut. She went looking for the children and she found three of them lying on a mattress in an upstairs room and they had all had their throats cut.

Mrs Kidnew went for assistance but during her absence another neighbour had entered the house and found the fourth child behind a bedroom door, also with his throat cut. A medical person was sent for and the police were informed. When these two arrived at the house it was found that Mrs Laycock and all four of the children were dead. The prisoner was found and although his throat was cut he was not dead, and near to his hand were found an ordinary table knife and a candlestick. Mrs Laycock and the children were removed and taken to the mortuary and the prisoner was taken to the

Sheffield hospital. While being conveyed there the prisoner had said "It's all through drink. It occurred at 12 o'clock". Mr Fenwick opened the statement by saying to the jury that there could be no doubt that he had committed the murder and if they were satisfied on that point it was their duty to say whether the prisoner was conscious of the crime that he had committed.

(You will notice that the details of the finding of the bodies in this report by The Times newspaper differs slightly from their report published on the 12th July, but we can assume that the reporting of the trial gives the most accurate account).

Then it was time for the defence, and Mr. Meysey-Thompson stood up to make their case. He started by saying that at the time that the murders were committed the prisoner was not competent to understand what he was doing. He told the jury that he would call evidence to put before them to prove this and to show what had been the previous history of the prisoner's family. Witnesses would be called before them who would tell them that for some days before the 10th of July the prisoner was in a depressed state of mind. Evidence would also be called to show that when the prisoner was a child he suffered from some affliction of the brain. Then he called the defence witnesses.

The first to take the stand was the Sheffield Hospital surgeon Mr. St.Clair White. He said that he saw the prisoner when he was brought into the hospital with his throat cut. He was suffering from extreme mental depression. The prisoner had begged him to let him die, and asked him to cut his throat deeper. He was of the opinion that the prisoner was incapable of judging the nature of the crime that he had committed.

The second defence witness was a file cutter who knew the prisoner's father. He said that the man had committed suicide about ten years earlier by throwing himself into the River Don and drowning. He also knew three of the prisoner's uncles. Their names were William, John and Richard. William had died a natural death, John had cut his own throat and Richard had committed suicide by lying on the tracks of the railway.

Joseph's sister, Elizabeth Platts was called next to testify in defence of her brother. She said that on the Monday before the 10th of July Joseph had come to see her at her shop in Sheffield. She said that he seemed "lost" and did not seem to be "right in his mind".

Then Joseph's mother took the stand. Her name was Sarah Spilling and she told the court that the prisoner was her son by her first husband. She said that Joseph had suffered from brain fever in his childhood, and had undergone medical treatment for the disease.

Two more witnesses were called, Michael Allan and Selina Hudson also testified in regard to Joseph's depressed condition in the few days before the murders.

The case for the defence was then closed and the judge summed up for the jury. He opened by saying that there was no subject which involved greater difficulty than in deciding on the mental health of a man charged with murder. The very atrociousness of the crime suggested that it was not the act of a sane man, but there might be motives which they could not fathom, and which were not disclosed to them. He commented on a lack of medical evidence and said it would be better if such cases as they were trying were referred to some public functionary. The duty of that official should be to investigate the cases, and to furnish the best possible medical evidence. He hoped there would be some alteration in the matter. His Lordship then dealt with the evidence of the case at considerable length after which the jury retired to consider their verdict. It took them only twenty minutes to return with a verdict of Guilty. Joseph was asked by the Clerk of Arraigns whether he had anything to say as to why the sentence of death should not be passed upon him. He made no reply.

The judge then donned the black cap and said "I will not add to the terror and misery of your position by one word of comment on the terrible tragedy of which you have been convicted. It is my duty to pass upon you the sentence of the law and he sentenced him to death. The judge was about to leave the bench when Joseph exclaimed "Thank you, your worship, thank you".

His execution date was set for the 26th of August 1884. On the evening before, his mother and a couple of other relatives went to visit him and found him in better spirits than they had expected. He said that he was looking forward to being in a better place and hoping that he would see them again - urging them to live a good life so that they would be prepared when it came their time to leave this world. The authorities confirmed that he seemed to be in fairly good spirits on the evening before the execution, but his nerve had failed him when the morning came. He fainted in his cell and had to be held upright by two warders as he walked to the scaffold which had been erected in the prison yard. His last words before he was hanged were "Oh my children, my children. Lord have mercy on my children." Despite the horrible crime that he committed, many people spoke of how much he had loved his children and how he had always been kind and gentle with them. No one can dispute the fact that it was a terrible crime. The jury had no sympathy for him whatsoever and it took them only twenty minutes to deliver a guilty verdict. The judge however was somewhat uneasy about the situation. When a man was convicted of such a horrendous crime as this one, a judge would usually leave the defendant in no doubt whatsoever about how wicked he was but the judge didn't say anything like that. He said "I will not add to the terror and misery of your position by one word of comment on the terrible tragedy of which you have been convicted". He was acknowledging Joseph's terror and misery and described what had happened as a terrible tragedy, not as a wicked crime. I have great respect for the insight and compassion of this judge.

He also voiced his concerns about the lack of comprehensive medical evidence regarding Joseph's mental health. His concerns echoed beyond this case which was in front of him and he suggested the need for the creation of a dedicated body to assess and guide courts in cases such as this one. It was a rare moment of introspection and wisdom in an era that often dismissed mental illness as moral failing or weakness.

Joseph's case, tragic and horrifying as it was, underscored the urgent need for progress in how society and the justice system approached mental health. His story serves as a stark reminder of the lives that can be lost not only to violence but also by the failure to understand and address the complexities of the human mind.

A horrified neighbour finds the murdered body of Maria
Laycock

Joseph Laycock lying seriously injured after trying to commit suicide. His murdered children lie on mattresses behind him. The murder weapon is on the floor next to

Joseph

CHAPTER FIVE: 1905. Harold Walters. The first man to be hanged in Wakefield Prison

WALTERS.

I wrote in Chapter One about William Smedley, the last Sheffield man to be hanged. In this chapter we look at another "claim to fame" that Sheffield could do without. It was a Sheffield man called Harold Walters who was the first person to be hanged at Wakefield Prison. Nicknamed "Monster Mansion" it is the UK's largest high-security prison, housing some of the country's most dangerous criminals. It didn't house Harold (Harry) Walters for long of course because in 1905 the mandatory sentence for murder was death by hanging. It would seem that the cause of Walters' downfall was the demon drink because according to Wakefield Prison records he was cited for drunkenness eleven times between 1895 and 1905. Available records don't show where Walters was living during those ten years, but in October 1905 he moved into 12 Court, 7 House, Allen Street, Sheffield with his girlfriend Sarah Ann McConnell. At 39 years of age he was four years younger than Sarah, who had separated from her husband some time before she set up home with Walters. If they were both happy with their new living arrangements it didn't last long because tragedy would strike within a couple of months. On the afternoon of Saturday the 23rd of December 1905 a woman called Margaret Revill knocked on their door trying to sell them some fish. Sarah said that they didn't want any and turned to go back inside. Presumably Mrs Revill had interrupted an argument between the pair because as she turned to leave she heard Walters tell Sarah that he would kill her as soon as the fish seller had gone. If only Sarah had taken her opportunity to escape and go with Margaret Revill she would have escaped the horror that she was about to endure. We can only assume that arguments and threats to kill her were not unusual as it would seem that she did not take the threat seriously. At about 5.30 that same evening, the landlord Jane Drakard called at their home to collect the rent. She had an assistant with her. The scene that met the rent collectors was completely horrific. Sarah was lying almost naked on the rug in front of the fire with her legs apart and blood streaming from her vagina. Jane and her assistant covered Sarah with her skirt which was lying nearby and rushed to find help.

While they were away an eleven year old girl called Margaret Osbourne called to collect some money that Sarah owed her mother. The door had been left open when the rent collectors rushed off to get help and Margaret could see the dreadful scene inside. She saw Walters kneeling beside Sarah's unconscious body and calling her name in a vain attempt to wake her up. He left with Margaret and went with her to her mother's house and asked the woman to go and stay with Sarah while he went in search of a policeman. He returned shortly afterwards with PC Winfield. The policeman saw a blood stained beer bottle and a blood stained broom handle beside Sarah's body.

His trial began at the Quarter Sessions in Leeds on the 23rd of March 1906. He pleaded Not Guilty to the charge of murder. The prosecution outlined the details of the crime and said that when he was arrested his clothing was very heavily blood-stained. Walters denied that he had had anything at all to do with the murder and said that the bloodstains must have got onto his clothes as he knelt beside Sarah. The jury were having none of it and took only 30 minutes to find him guilty. The judge donned the black cap and gave Walters the death penalty.

He was transported back to Wakefield prison to await his fate. At 9.30 a.m. on the 10th of April 1906 he was escorted out of the condemned cell and taken to the scaffold where he was hanged by Henry Pierrepoint.

CHAPTER SIX. The murder of Annie Cotterill in 2013

Harold Walters may have been the first man to be hanged in the newly opened Wakefield Prison, but another Sheffield man was also in the top ten. George Frederick Law was number 7 in the "Top Ten", when he was hanged in December 1913 for the murder of Annie Cotterill.

It seems that 34 year old George, a forge man, had been having an affair with 45 year old Annie Cotterill for about four years when he moved in to live with her and her husband as a lodger in their home at 17 Bamforth Street in Hillsborough in 1911.

All seemed to work quite well for a couple of years or so, until October 1913 when George was told that he would have to leave. The living arrangements in the house were not ideal. The house was a "two-up, two-down" and to accommodate George, he had to sleep in the same bedroom as Annie's husband and Annie had to share a bedroom with their daughter. The daughter was planning to get married and maybe the plan was for her and her husband to move in and live with her parents. Or maybe Annie's husband had finally found out after six years that George and Annie were having sex behind his back.

George ignored the request to leave, so on Monday the 21st of October he was given formal written notice that he had to leave. When both men returned from work that day George asked Annie's husband why he had given him notice to leave. "You know very well, George, what I have given you notice for, We want the house to ourselves as the daughter is getting married.". George then jumped up from the couch and said, sarcastically, "Thank you very much" and made vague threats of violence before storming out of the house. The husband, naturally concerned, decided it would be wise to hide George's three razors and also his own.

George came back later that night, very drunk, and went up to sleep in the shared room. He asked where his razors were and when he was told that they had been removed for safety reasons he said that he had something sharper than them, and that there were two in the house that he would kill. Then he went downstairs into the yard and started vomiting. All the shouting and commotion woke up Annie and she, her husband and their daughter lay awake all night fearing for their lives.

The next morning George got dressed in his work clothes and went out as though he was going to work, but he didn't. He waited nearby watching until he was sure that Annie's husband and daughter had left the house and then he went back in and strangled Annie with a scarf and slashed her repeatedly about the head; apparently with a carving knife. With the terrible deed finished he took off his bloodstained working clothes, hid them under his bed, and dressed in his best Sunday suit and went to a local pub for a brandy and soda. Then he went to his sister's house in Nottingham.

Annie's husband found his wife lying dead on her bed when he got home from work that evening. It was obvious that Annie had fought hard for her life because several of her fingers had been cut and fractured.

Unsurprisingly the police were in no doubt about who had most likely committed the murder and they went to his sister's house and arrested him later that same night. When he was arrested he said to the police "What I did to Annie this morning I did in a temper. Is she dead? I have been expecting you". In his pocket they found the written notice to quit that he had been issued with and also a piece of paper on which had been written "Please withdraw the notice or it will be made worse for you. From G.F. Law. The end of this."

In notes taken by the police there were suggestions that there was trouble between Annie and her husband because of George Law, but this was not brought up in court. On the contrary, at the trial Annie's husband said that there was no reason for giving George his notice. He said "Nothing particular, only my wife and I thought we would give notice". George's plea of insanity was rejected and he was sentenced to death with no recommendation to mercy. He was returned to Wakefield prison to await his fate. He appealed the sentence but it was denied.

There was then a medical inquiry into his mental condition and a detailed report was written on the 23rd of December 1913. The report stated that during a very long interview he eventually revealed details of his relationship with Annie Cotterill and told how he had committed the crime. George had told the medical officer that he had become friendly with Annie and her husband some time before he went to lodge with them, and that Annie had succeeded in inciting him to have a sexual relationship with her and that the relationship had continued until the morning before the murder - a period of six years. He also said that not only did he have natural sexual intercourse with her but that he also frequently practised masturbation on her at her instigation. He said that she was also intimate with other men but that he didn't mind that. He said that her husband and daughter were aware of his relationship with Annie.

He told the medical officer that on the morning of the murder, Tuesday the 21st of October, he had dressed in his work clothes and left the house as though he was going to work, but he waited and watched until her husband and daughter had left the house and had then gone back in. He went up to Annie's bedroom. *(Maybe he had done this on a regular basis. He had told the medical officer that the last time he had had sex with Annie was on the morning before the murder. It seems likely that he went up to Annie's bedroom on the morning of the murder for sex, and probably for reassurance from her that she would use her feminine wiles to persuade her husband to withdraw the notice to quit. If that was his intention and hope he was to be very sadly disappointed and when Annie told him so he killed her.)*

His account to the medical officer continued: He said that when he got to Annie's bedroom she told him to "Clear out and go quietly". This had finally convinced him that Annie was really anxious to be rid of him and he had become extremely angry. He was also anxious and distressed by the thought that his libidinous practices might be made known to the neighbours and that he would become a disgrace so he decided that he needed to put her out of the way.

He said that he seized her by the throat with his right hand and that she had murmured "Oh Lord" and that he continued his attack by tying his scarf around her neck and then beating her about the head with a knotted stick.

He was hanged at Wakefield prison by Thomas Pierrepoint on the 31st of December 1913. Newspapers reported that he walked calmly and quietly to the scaffold.

CHAPTER SEVEN: 1900 The murder of Walter Hague

Times change and when you look into the circumstances of a crime you need to take into account when it happened and what the social norms that society lived by were at the time. I think that, if 23 year old Walter Hague had been murdered today, the perpetrator would have been immediately identified, arrested, charged and found guilty of murder. But the murder didn't happen today, it happened in 1900 and the perpetrator got away with it. The case is presented as a mystery and an unsolved crime, which it may be, but I think that if you look at the crime through a 1900 lens it is reasonably obvious what probably happened.

The date was Saturday the 22nd of September 1900 and Walter went to the Carlton Hotel /pub on Attercliffe to meet his fiancee Alice Basford. Alice worked there as a waitress/ barmaid and finished work at 11 pm. The pair had been estranged from each other for quite   a while but Walter had contacted her the previous Saturday and she had agreed to meet him on this Saturday. It was a dark miserable rainy night. He collected her at the Carlton Hotel and the two of them set off to walk the mile or so from the pub to the Midland Station on Sheaf Street to catch a train to travel together to Alice's home in Darnall.

The path up to the station was even darker than the streets, and the two were sharing the same umbrella as they hurried to make sure that they did not miss their train. As they walked they passed a man who was obviously drunk and was swearing and cursing about some issue that was obviously upsetting him. They had already passed him slightly earlier and had ignored him and they ignored him again as they hurried to get out of the rain, into the station and onto the platform to get their train.

Suddenly without warning the drunken man came up behind Walter, put his arms around his neck, punched him hard in the chest and kicked him as he fell to the ground. The man then ran off. Apparently unhurt, Walter got to his feet and said that he wished that a policeman had been around so that the man could have been arrested and taken into custody. He asked Alice to brush the dust from his clothes but then simply said "Oh" before falling to the ground as a shocked and horrified Alice shouted for help. It was soon apparent that Walter had not been punched in the chest; he had been stabbed and the knife had gone into his heart. Walter had been fatally wounded and died almost immediately.

Two days later, Sheffield police arrested a man on suspicion of committing the murder. The man is called George Donovan in some reports and James Donovan in others so I will refer to him throughout by his surname, Donovan. They released him without charge after questioning him for five hours and did not seem to have any other leads to follow. The reason for suspecting and arresting Donovan is not clear, but I have my own idea about why that might have been which I will describe later.

Two weeks later, on Monday the 8th of October, 38 year-old Donovan went into the Parliament Street police station in Hull between 11 and 12 pm and told the desk officer that he was wanted by Sheffield police for the murder of Walter Hague. Although Donovan lived in Sheffield he worked periodically as a marine engineer and he had been in Hull for the past week trying to get a position on a boat leaving from Hull, but without success.

He was taken into a back room and interviewed by a senior officer. He told the officer that he had recently started a relationship with a Sheffield woman and on the day in question, Saturday the 22nd of September they had met up during the day and he had bought her a bonnet. They had arranged to meet each other after she finished work at 11 pm that night and catch a train to Hull together. Before meeting her, he had had a lot to drink but he went and met her as arranged and they started walking together towards the Midland station to catch the train. As they walked, he realised that his lady friend was nowhere to be seen so he continued on towards the station looking for her. As he got near to the station he thought that he saw her, but she was not alone; she was in the company of another man. He approached the couple with the intention of asking the woman what was happening with a view to asking her to join him to go and catch their train as planned. He said that the man that she was with resented the intrusion and that he thought that the man was going to attack him. To defend himself, and with no intention of causing any serious harm to the man, he drew out his knife and stabbed him. He said that he lost his hat in the struggle and then ran away and remained in Sheffield all night. He later returned to Hull and the matter was on his conscience so he decided that the best thing he could do was to give himself up to the authorities and put an end to the matter. He also said that the Hull police could not do anything to him because they had had him for it once, at Sheffield. His confession was taken down in writing and he signed it.

Donovan was very mistaken about the police not being able to do anything about it, and he was transferred to Sheffield the next day, where he was remanded in custody on suspicion of the murder of Walter Hague. Donovan was now having serious concerns about what might happen as a result of his confession so he said that he had been coerced into making the confession, with the police keeping him awake questioning him all night and not allowing him to sleep. He did though stick to the fact that he had had an altercation with someone and had attacked him.

He was brought up before the magistrates the next day and charged with wilful murder and remanded pending a court hearing at the Leeds Assizes. Before the court hearing, the judge said that he felt that there was probably insufficient evidence to find Donovan guilty of murder. Although several witnesses had testified at the magistrates' hearing that they thought that Donovan looked like the man who had killed Hague, no-one had made a completely positive identification. He also said that there was reason to believe that Hague was the aggressor and that Donovan had acted to defend himself. In that situation the charge would have to be manslaughter and not murder. However he decided that he would allow the jury to be the ones who would consider the matter and Donovan was tried at the Leeds Assizes.

The prosecution opened their case by describing the events of the 22nd September; the night when Walter Hague had been stabbed to death. They said that witnesses would confirm that on that evening he had been drinking in the Bay Horse Inn on Greystock Street from 8 pm until 10.30. A drunken man who was swearing was seen in the Sheaf Street area at about 11.15 pm and the prosecution contended that this was the defendant and that he was lying in wait for Walter Hague and Alice Basford. When Walter and Alice arrived at the station, he attacked and stabbed Walter who died more or less instantly.

Two days later, the Sheffield police had arrested him and questioned him for five hours but released him without charge. They described how he had gone into a police station in Hull a couple of weeks later and confessed to the crime; a confession that he subsequently claimed had been coerced out of him by the Hull police.

The prosecution said that the questions that the jury would need to consider were: Was the prisoner the man who attacked Hague, and if so, were the circumstances sufficient to suggest wilful murder or only manslaughter? Then they called their first witness, who was the Hull police officer who had questioned Donovan on the night that he went to the police station and confessed to the crime.

Next to give evidence was Alice Basford. She said that she had not had a proper look at the man who had stabbed Walter, and agreed that on more than one occasion she had attended identity parades and been asked to identify the assailant. When asked whether she had picked out Donovan she replied that she had picked him out "as well as she could from the descriptions that she had heard of him". At another identity parade she had picked out a serving police officer!

Various people who had witnessed the crime were called but although some said that Donovan resembled the assailant, nobody could positively identify him.

No defence witnesses were called because the judge had heard enough by this point. As no-one had been able to positively identify the defendant as the man who had killed Walter Hague, and his confession could not be relied on he said that there was no point in proceeding any further. He said that the jury could not possibly be expected to convict the defendant on the available evidence. The jury therefore returned a verdict of "Not Guilty" and Donovan was discharged. No more was heard in the public domain about Donovan or Alice Basford and no-one else was ever charged with the murder of Walter Hague.

The case is presented as a mystery but I think that there are clues that suggest the answers to the questions that remain:

Donovan maintained that he had started a relationship with Alice Basford during the period preceding the murder when she had been estranged from Walter Hague. In 1900 respectable society had very strict rules about how young women were expected to behave. They were supposed to dress in a demure way and remain a virgin until their wedding night. Much opprobrium was heaped onto the shoulders of any poor soul who breached these rules. Although she and Walter had been somewhat estranged for a period before the murder, the pair were officially engaged, and she presented herself at Donovan's trial as the fiancee of Walter Hague. In his confession, Donovan had said that he had been in a relationship with Alice. She was a woman who was still engaged to another man and so this would have been a completely unacceptable situation in 1900. The prosecutor at the trial put the question to her in a polite manner when he said "I suppose there is not the slightest truth in the suggestion that you have met this man before?" Maybe fearing a charge of perjury if a witness was called who would testify to there having been a relationship between her and Donovan she replied "No, not to my knowledge". The question was not "Have you ever met this man before". It referred to whether there was any truth in the suggestion that she had met Donovan before. The only place that that suggestion had come from was in Donovan's confession where he had said that they had had a relationship.

She had also been asked at the inquest about whether she had been in any sort of relationship with Donovan, although there is no specific information about the question and answer but the newspapers noted that she had told the inquest that there could be "no suggestion of jealousy" being the cause of the murder.

The other puzzle is why the Sheffield police questioned Donovan two days after the murder. Maybe his explanation at the Magistrate's Court about why he went to the Hull police station and confessed to the murder holds the answer to this. He told the magistrates that he went to the police station to "explain the matter, and to stop people talking". One has to ask what they were talking about. It is highly unlikely that he and Alice could have been seeing each other without people knowing. She worked as a waitress/barmaid in a pub and people in the bar would have seen them together. I would suggest that people had talked to the police and told them about the fact that Donovan and Alice appeared to be in a relationship together and that that is why he was arrested and questioned. His answers must have satisfied them because he was released without charge.

When Donovan retracted his confession he did stick to the fact that he had had an altercation with someone and attacked him. This is a very strange thing for him to do and there were no reports of anyone else having been attacked by him, so why he would do that remains a bit of a mystery.

Neither Donovan or Walter Hague had any sort of criminal past. It is my view that jealousy was the cause of the murder. Whether Walter was the instigator of the altercation and Donovan acted in self defence or whether in his drunken state, Donovan was angry and jealous of the fact that Alice had gone back to her fiance and the jealousy led to the murder. It's impossible to say.

These are just my thoughts based on what I have read about the case. Other than jealousy, I can see no reason for two hard working men who had no history of violence or crime to get into this altercation that led to the death of such a young man. I leave it to readers to form their own opinions.

An artist's depiction of the murder of Walter Hague

CHAPTER EIGHT: Unsolved Murders

Officially, the murder of Walter Hague is an unsolved murder although, in my opinion there is evidence to show that Donovan committed the crime. There are many murders in Sheffield and elsewhere that are "unsolved". Many of them are unsolved because the perpetrator got away with the murder, but with others the suspect was tried and found "Not Guilty" by a jury and because the police and the prosecution considered that they had correctly identified and tried their suspect they made no further enquiries.

In this chapter, we look at a couple more unsolved murders.

The Murder of Mary Anne Elliott on Saturday 26th March 1921

Forty-three year old Mary Anne lived with her husband and four children at 38 Abney Street, Sheffield. Like many a married woman before her and since she was having an affair. Her lover was a soldier who lived at 61 Fawcett Street in Sheffield although at the time of the murder he was stationed at the York and Lancaster Regiment in Pontefract.

It was common practice in the early 20th century for families who had a spare room to rent it out to a lodger and the Elliott family were no different and they rented a room in their home to a female lodger called Pollie. Mary confided in Pollie about her affair and she agreed that he could send letters to Mary but addressed to her. I would guess that, if she didn't want to lose her tenancy of the room, she had little choice but to agree whether she was happy with the situation or not.

On the 26th of March 1921 Mary was found dead in a pool of blood in Portobello Street Sheffield. Her throat had been cut so severely that she was almost decapitated.

The police started their enquiries and Pollie said that Mary's husband had not known anything about his wife's affair. Presumably she was just trying to protect Mary's husband because the police soon learned that he did in fact know about what was going on between his wife and the soldier. The couple's two sons and Pollie said that the husband had returned home at about 10 pm on the night of the murder and remained at home until the police had come and told him of the death of his wife.

At the soldier's later trial, it was alleged that about a year earlier when Mary and her husband were out together they had met the soldier. It was obvious that her husband suspected that something was going on between the pair because he asked the soldier "what his game was". A row developed and the soldier said that he was going to get a solicitor and the husband shot back "You can get two!" The soldier said that he would "have Mary ". She protested that she didn't understand what the soldier had meant about getting a solicitor or his remark about "having her". Maybe this calmed the situation down, but the seeds had been sown. Her husband clearly knew that something was going on between his wife and the soldier.

Pollie told the police that the letters from the soldier, which were always addressed to her, were posted in Pontefract and they had begun arriving about six months before the murder. Mary had shown her two of them and they were love letters. The last letter from the soldier had been in March and he had not sent a letter or a card for her at Easter.

She said that Mary drank a lot and that since the start of her affair with the soldier she had been staying out late quite frequently.

She herself worked as a waitress and was on her way home from work on the night of the murder and she had actually passed the place where the murder happened about twenty minutes before the body was discovered. She had not seen anyone about or anything at all unusual.

A man told the police that he had seen Mary with the soldier drinking in the White Hart pub in Solly Street at about 9.15 pm on the night in question and that the pair had left at the same time that he did which was about 10 pm When they left the couple set off walking in the direction of St George's church. He had left and walked in the opposite direction.

A woman out with her husband that night said that she had seen Mary talking to two men in Siddall Street at about 10.30 pm. She and her husband said that one of the men was a civilian and the other was a soldier.

It was a police constable walking his beat who actually discovered the body. It was 11.40 pm and he saw a man running away from the doorway of what is now Laycocks Works on Portobello Street. He had been about thirty yards from the man who had obviously seen him approaching and set off running. He gave chase but stopped when he got to the doorway of the Works and found Marie's body lying there. Unfortunately he had not seen how the man was dressed and could not therefore say whether or not he was dressed as a soldier. He said that the woman was still breathing despite her terrible injury and was lying on her right side with her head resting on her arm. Her clothing had not been disturbed .

Her body was taken to the mortuary and a letter was found in her pocket. It was addressed to the lodger and it said:

Dear Pollie love,

On Saturday night I shall be eagerly looking forward to seeing you love. It seems ages since I saw you last. I have been at school all the morning sitting for an examination for my third class certificate. I now finish with my best love.

Your ever sincere and faithful sweetheart. Goodnight and God bless.

Xxxxxxx   P.S. Some real ones tomorrow love.

A police sergeant went to examine the scene as soon as it was light the next day and under the doorway where the body had been he found a silver gilt ring with a buckle. At the soldier's later trial the sergeant was shown twelve rings to see whether or not he was able to identify the ring that he had found. He identified it easily. Two privates stationed at Pontefract identified the ring as having belonged to the soldier. One of them said that he had given the ring to the soldier and had seen him wearing it. As with the police sergeant they had both identified the ring from the twelve rings shown to them by the police.

The pathologist who carried out the post mortem on Mary's body said that the wound to her throat was six and a half inches long and that she would have lived only a few minutes after receiving it.

At the inquest into her death the soldier said that he did not murder Mary and that he was willing to go into the witness box but the Coroner would not allow him or his father to give evidence. He said that it was better that they get legal advice about the matter. He also said that he did not find the evidence about the ring to be conclusive evidence that the soldier had murdered Mary. He said that the soldier had been in her company that evening and might have given it to her as a gift. Finding the ring at the scene was not evidence that the soldier had ever been there. He also commented on the fact that no weapon had been found and that, in his view, the evidence against the soldier was far from satisfactory.

The soldier was tried at Leeds Assizes on the 6th of May 1922 and found Not Guilty. That is, of course, the proper verdict if the evidence didn't show beyond all reasonable doubt that he had murdered Mary but it doesn't mean that he didn't do it, and I think that the evidence suggests that maybe he did.

Before explaining why I think that, it is necessary to rule out the probability that her husband murdered her. It seems apparent that Mary's husband had known (or at least had strong suspicions) about the affair for at least a year, and it could be said that he therefore had a motive to murder her, but many men find out that their wife is having an affair but very few of them commit murder because of it. On the night of the murder Mary's two sons, and Pollie said that Mary's husband was home by about 10pm on that night and didn't go out again. He was at home when the police went to inform him about the murder of his wife. Obviously, if he had murdered Mary he could not have been home by 10pm because the murder was committed at about 11.40. If he was the murderer, the earliest that he could have been home in Abney Street was 11.50 pm because the distance between Portobello Street and Abney Street is only about half a mile. The murder was very brutal and the person who had committed it would have been covered in blood. I don't think that it's realistic to think that the husband arrived home at almost midnight covered in blood and that his sons and Pollie lied for him when the police arrived not long afterwards to tell them about the murder. It's possible, but extremely unlikely in my opinion.

I think that we can also rule out the likelihood that a stranger murdered Mary. She was fully dressed and had not been sexually assaulted and she was found in the open, on a street that had people passing along it at frequent intervals - not a suitable place to commit a murder in order to rape or sexually assault a woman.

That leaves us with the question as to whether the soldier murdered Mary. A witness had said that he had been in the White Hart pub on the evening of the murder and that Mary and the soldier had left at about 10 pm and walked in the direction of St George's church on St George's Terrace so the couple were heading in the right direction to reach Portobello Street. The next recorded sighting of the couple was at 10.30 pm on Siddall Street. Witnesses said that Mary was talking with two men, a soldier and a civilian. We can reasonably assume that the soldier and Mary were together as a couple and that they had stopped to chat to a man in civilian clothes. Siddall Street is almost one and a half miles from Portobello Street. It would take a couple walking at a leisurely pace about 45 minutes to walk that distance. If Mary and the soldier chatted with the man in civilian clothes for 15 minutes or so they would arrive at the murder site in Portobello Street at about 11.30 pm. There must have been an argument there and in the struggle, the soldier lost his ring, which was found at the scene.

It was about a ten minute walk from Portobello Street to the soldier's home on Fawcett Street, and a similar ten minute walk in a different direction from Portobello Street to Mary's home on Abney Street. Presumably the couple would have parted there on Portobello Street and gone their separate ways home, but something happened and he murdered Mary. Maybe it was a sudden argument or maybe he had had it planned that he would murder her.

The soldier's father said that he himself had gone to bed between 10 and 11 pm that night and that his son had arrived home at about 11.30 pm. He said that he had never seen Mary Elliott and had known nothing about a relationship between her and his son. This may seem like an alibi but I would suggest that it was not. The father was in bed and heard his son come in at "about 11.30". The police constable saw the murderer running from the scene at 11.40 pm. It was a ten minute walk from the scene of the murder to the soldier's home, but he was not walking he was running and, as a soldier he would be very physically fit. He would have been home not long after 11.40 and his father was telling the truth when he said that his son arrived home at "about 11.30".

I would say that there are a couple of things to consider when suggesting that the soldier murdered Mary. There is the question of motive. The pair seemed to be friendly towards each other when they were seen during that evening, but that does not rule him out. A more serious problem is the issue of his soldier's uniform. There is no doubt that he was wearing his uniform that evening. Witnesses saw him, and his father also told the police that his son had been wearing his uniform. That uniform would have been soaked in blood. He could not have destroyed it by throwing it into the coal fire in his living room as other murderers have done in the past because how would he account for it being missing? So maybe that rules him out. Despite that issue, the police and prosecution obviously thought he was the killer and put him on trial. When the jury found him Not Guilty no-one else was ever arrested or tried.

The murder of John Henry Wortley on Thursday 5th June 1975.

If there was any doubt about the motive for the murders of Walter Hague and Mary Anne Cotterill there is none about the murder of 66 year old John Henry Wortley on the 6th of June 1975. It was robbery; pure and simple.

He was not due to work on the 5th of June, and I'm sure that he went as did millions of other UK citizens to cast his vote on whether or not the United Kingdom should stay in the European Economic Community (EEC). At the age of 66 he had already retired from his job as a night attendant at the NCP multi storey car park on Arundel Gate, but he kept himself busy doing occasional shifts when asked. No doubt he was looking forward to enjoying the rest of the day off, but he was contacted and asked if he could cover a shift that night and, as always, he was happy to step in and oblige. The big national news the next day was that the electorate had voted overwhelmingly in favour of remaining in the European Economic Community (EEC) in the previous day's national Referendum. The big news for the people of Sheffield was that a night attendant in a City centre car park had been murdered. He had been seen alive working in his kiosk on the first level of the car park at 8.18 pm and he was found battered to death by a driver who stopped at the kiosk five minutes later at 8.23 pm.   The murder weapon was a fire extinguisher which was lying beside him covered in blood. His killer had obviously beat him mercilessly over the head with it.

Police soon arrived and determined that the motive for the murder was robbery because between £50 and £70 was missing from the till. A major police investigation was launched, but despite their best efforts and a £1000 reward for information the killer was never found and this remains an unsolved mystery.

People told reporters that John, a loving father and grandfather was well known and liked in his community. He was always helpful and kept an eye out for my neighbours who might need a helping hand. After the murder, John's wife told reporters that she hoped that her husband's murder would haunt the killer for the rest of his life. I hope so too, but I think it's unlikely that a man who could murder a kind and defenceless man for a small amount of money will suffer any pangs of conscience.

CHAPTER NINE: The Death of Russian Edna in 1954

As we saw in Chapter Two with the murder of Edith
Simmonite, making a living as a prostitute is a very
precarious business. The prostitute known as Russian Edna
is one of those sad souls who seem to become well known as
a prostitute around their area. Maybe she was better known
than most other prostitutes because we have a painting in
our house by Sheffield artist George Cunningham called
"Two Free Houses" which shows a city centre street scene.
The bottom right corner of the painting shows a woman
walking arm in arm with a man and I am told that this
woman is Russian Edna, presumably walking with a "client"
of hers. It seems that the reason that she became well known
in the City was her colourful clothing and eccentric
personality.

What her real name was is hard to say. She was born in
Russia in 1901 and known by everybody as "Russian Edna".
The authorities referred to her real name as being Malanie
Birch, but that doesn't sound very Russian to me, so who
knows? The circumstances that brought her to England, and
to live in Sheffield are not clear. Records show that she had
married a soldier but the marriage floundered and she was
left to cope alone. It's unlikely that she had any family to
help or support her and so left to fend for herself she did
what many women in similar sad circumstances did, and
turned to prostitution.

On Monday the 15th of March 1954, 52 year old Edna appeared before the Sheffield Magistrates Court. This wasn't unusual for her and, whatever the charge was, she was found guilty and given the option of going to prison or paying a £5 fine within 7 days. This is equivalent to about £169 pounds today. Edna chose the option of the £5 fine rather than the prison sentence. This does seem to me to be a very harsh choice because it would be extremely difficult for a person in Edna's situation to find £5 within 7 days, in addition to her usual expenses of lodging and food. It would seem that she was doing her best however because on Monday the 22nd of March she had paid a contribution towards the fine into the courthouse. The tragic events that would soon unfold suggest that after making this payment she still had to find another £2 urgently if she was to avoid being sent to prison for failing to pay the full fine within 7 days. If she was counting the 7 days as starting on the day after her sentencing, she needed to get the outstanding £2 to the court the next day if she was to avoid prison.

That evening found her plying her trade at one of her usual haunts, The Sportsman Public House on Cambridge Street. Before long she had found a willing client and the two of them caught a taxi to High Hazel's Park in Tinsley; a short distance from her home in Darnall Road.. Edna knew that there was a public shelter at the back of the park where she could provide her client with the service that he had agreed to pay her for without anyone seeing them.

Her dead body was found the next morning by two miners who were walking through the park and the police were called. Their enquiries at the Sportsman pub soon provided them with a suspect. The Yorkshire Post ran an article on Wednesday the 24 of March, the day after her body was found. It read:

"Sheffield police wish to interview a 24 year old lorry driver, a native of Leeds, who bites his fingernails. They believe he can help them in their inquiries into the death of 52 year old Melanie Birch (known as Russian Edna) whose body was found in a public shelter in High Hazels Park Sheffield at about 6 a.m. on Tuesday. A description of the man, George William Pullan, has been circulated to police forces throughout the country. It is as follows:

'Height 5ft. 9 in., proportionate build, fresh complexion, brown hair, blue eyes, slight scar over left eye and another on left side of nose; wears spectacles and bites his nails. May be dressed in brown coloured sports jacket, brown checked pattern shirt and blue trousers. It is understood that Pullan has lived in Sheffield for some years."

While the police searched for their suspect the Sheffield Coroner, Mr A. P. Lockwood opened the inquest into Edna's death on Wednesday the 24th of March. Her official name of Melanie Birch was used. The only evidence heard was from Detective Chief Inspector Thompson who was in charge of the case. He said that the woman, aged 52, was also known as Rita. She was a registered alien and signed her name "Melanie Billing". She was born in Reval, Russia in 1901. She had never been naturalised and police records showed she had a number of convictions for various offences. The inquest was then adjourned until the 8th of April.

On Wednesday the 24th of March the police had put their nationwide alert to all police forces to look out for George Pullan and he was found the next day in nearby Rotherham by Police Sergeant Herbert Wigglesworth. Sgt. Wigglesworth, who was in plain clothes, was driving along the Rotherham Road between Canklow and Brinsworth when his headlights picked out the figure of a man walking along in the pouring rain. Thinking that he looked rather like the description of the wanted man he pulled up beside the man and offered him a lift. After driving for a short while Sgt. Wigglesworth asked the man his name and he replied that it was William. The police officer replied "I think your name is Pullen" and Pullen replied "That's it". He was taken to Rotherham Police Station and then to the Sheffield Magistrates Court the following morning. He told the Court:

"I didn't know I had killed her. I didn't know her name was Melanie Birch; I knew her as Russian Edna. She tried to blackmail me. I had agreed to pay her £1 and she later demanded £2. She said that if I didn't pay up she would scream out and say I had attacked her, so I put my hand over her mouth".

Pullen's trial began at the Leeds Assizes on the 6th of July 1954. He pleaded Not Guilty to murder, but Guilty to Manslaughter. The prosecution did not accept this pleas, probably because pathologist Dr Gilbert Forbes had told the Magistrates Court that Edna had died of strangulation and that her neck would have had to be squeezed for at least four minutes.

Pullen told the Court that he had agreed to pay her £1 for sex but after they had finished she had said to him "Make it £2 now". I told her "I can't". (As I suggested earlier, I am guessing that Edna still owed the Court £2 of the fine she had been given. The deadline had passed the previous day and she would have been desperate to get the £2 to pay off the fine and avoid a jail sentence).

He continued "She said 'I'll scream and shout" and I heard men's voices coming. I moved my hands from under her and put one hand over her mouth to stop her shouting. She started struggling as the voices got near us. I put more pressure on her mouth, and when they'd gone away I said "Come on now. I'm off." She didn't answer me and I thought she was shamming. "I left her where she was on the ground and I walked into Darnall. The next day I realised what I had done. When I went out I bought the evening paper. I saw it on the front page that she'd been found dead."

After a two day trial the jury found him Not Guilty of Murder, but guilty of Manslaughter. The judge, Mr Justice Donovan passed a sentence of twelve months imprisonment. He said "The jury have taken the view which they are entitled to take - an accidental death, although unlawful killing. Unlawful killing it still remains."

When her body was found she had only one bent penny in her pocket. It is hard not to feel sorry for both Edna and Pullen. Edna's circumstances were desperate and I do think that she was trying to get the £2 she needed to avoid being sent to prison. Pullen was a young man who panicked when she threatened to scream that he had attacked her, and I doubt that he had any intention of doing Edna harm when he went into the shelter with her. He died in Scarborough

Woman found murdered in park
1954

From our Sheffield correspondent

Had Russian-born Melanie Birch aged 52 chosen to go to prison last week she would still have been alive. Instead Sheffield Magistrates allowed her a week in which to pay a £5 fine and yesterday morning, only a few hours after the time limit for payment had expired, she was found murdered in a wooden shelter in a Sheffield park.

At noon on Monday, the seventh day after being fined, she had gone to the Courthouse and paid something off the fine.

"She met her death by foul play. Robbery was not the motive," Chief Detective Inspector Thomas Butler, who with Chief Detective Inspector J. A. Thompson is in charge of the case, said last night. "We are checking up on her companions of Monday evening and would welcome any information as to her movements." He said he was not in a position at present to reveal the cause of death.

Two miners passing through High Hazels Park, only a mile from the woman's home in Darnall Road, found

Melanie Birch

the body and knocked up Mr William Preen, golf professional to the Tinsley Park Municipal Golf Club, who called the police.

'Russian Edna' Murder Charge

GEORGE WILLIAM WOOD PULLAN (24), unemployed lorry driver, Hall Road, Handsworth, Sheffield, was charged at Sheffield to-day with the murder of Melanie Birch (52), known as "Russian Edna," whose body was found in a public park shelter on Tuesday morning.

Detective-Chief Inspector J. A. Thompson, who brought Pullan from Rotherham, where he had been detained by the police last night, told the magistrates to-day that when Pullan was told of the discovery of the woman's body, he said:

"I didn't know I killed her. I didn't know her name was Melanie Birch. I knew her as 'Russian Edna.' She tried to blackmail me."

He went on to say that he had agreed to pay her £1 and she

CLOSING OF RURAL SCHOOLS

A memorandum, declaring the education committee's policy with regard to the closing down

in 1992. Edna is buried in Burngreave Cemetery.

Russian Edna who was murdered in High Hazels Park in 1954

CHAPTER TEN: The murder of Ada Bradley in 1923

How desperate would you have to be to throw a brick through a shop window just to get yourself arrested and thrown into prison for a rest? Luckily I am fortunate enough not to have to know, but thirty-one year old Rose Artliff certainly reached that point on an April morning in 1920. She had reached rock bottom. She was the mother of three young children and heavily pregnant with a fourth. These were the days before the welfare state and with no man to support her and unable to work due to her childcare responsibilities she had become destitute. She had sold all her furniture to pay debts and with unpaid rent and eviction staring her in the face she was in a very desperate situation. Rose had allegedly been married twice. According to census records she had married a plumber called George Barker in 1908 at the age of eighteen and they had three children together. There are no records to show that George and Rose had ever married and so it is likely that Rose was George's common law wife and not a legally married wife. The relationship broke down at some point and in 1916 he left Sheffield and moved to live in Nottingham. She was not on her own for long because in that same year she married 36 year old John Artliff and a baby was born to the couple the following year - 1917, but tragedy soon followed this happy event when Artliff died in that same year, leaving her on her own with four children to care for and support.

It's not clear what happened to her between 1917 and the day in April 1920 when she reached the end of her tether. We know that one of her children to George Barker, 9 year old Alice, died in 1919 and that in April 1920 she was heavily pregnant. Presumably she had had the support of the man whose child she was carrying for most of the time after John Artliff died but that relationship must have broken down leaving her to care for two of George Barker's children and her child to John Artliff.

She must have decided that her only hope was to go and see George in Nottingham, hoping that as he was the father of two of her children she might rekindle the relationship, or that at the very least he might provide her with some financial support. She got up on that morning in April 1920 and closing the front door behind her she left her three children alone inside the house. She went to her next door neighbour and gave her the very small amount of money that she had and asked her to keep an eye on the children until she returned.

She then set off to walk the 45 miles from Sheffield to Nottingham, and in her heavily pregnant state she managed to walk 30 miles to Mansfield before she knew that she could go no further. Without money to buy anything she decided to do the only thing that she could think of, which was to get herself arrested and put into prison. She threw a brick into a shop window, got arrested and spent one month in prison. Luckily her neighbour had informed the authorities that Rose's children had been left alone and they were admitted to the Fir Vale Workhouse.

When she was released from prison after serving her one month sentence the authorities expected that she would join her children in the Fir Vale Workhouse but it seems that she was still intent on finding George Barker in Nottingham because on the 29th of May 1920, shortly after being released from prison, she gave birth to a daughter in the Nottingham Workhouse. How she got to Nottingham after her failed attempt a month or so earlier is not recorded, but it is clear that, if she did find George Barker he was not interested in having anything to do with her or their two children. The baby was returned to Sheffield into the care of the authorities.

It seems that Rose's mental health was causing concerns at the Nottingham Workhouse because she was soon sent to the Wadsley Asylum in Sheffield where she was diagnosed as being depressed with suicidal tendencies, and possibly as also having homicidal tendencies.

(In 1948 the Wadsley Asylum changed its name and became the Middlewood Hospital. A massive sprawling building with quite a fearsome reputation. It received mentally ill patients from a very wide area and those who remember it (before it closed in 1996) only had to hear that someone was "In Middlewood" and we all knew exactly what it meant. Nobody had to say "What is Middlewood?", "Where is it?", "What service does it provide?". We all knew and hoped never to have to be admitted there.)

One of the nurses at the Asylum soon became close to Rose. Twenty year old Ada Bradley had had a much more fortunate life than Rose. She was born into a loving home and had earned herself a good job as a qualified nurse at the asylum. She was a friendly, cheerful young woman who was well liked by everyone, and given her kind nature she felt a lot of sympathy for Rose's desperate life story and befriended her. By December1921 the authorities decided that Rose was fit to be discharged, but where would she go? Ada decided that Rose should come and live with her at her parents' house which was a short distance away from the asylum. They had a spare room that they rented out but the man who had been lodging there for the last couple of years, twenty-two year old Walter Cooper, would be moving out in a couple of weeks time because he was joining the Coldstream Guards and moving to live in the Tower Hill Barracks in London. The authorities advised Ada that it was not a good idea to take Rose home with her, and it is likely that her parents had some misgivings, but Ada got her own way and Rose moved in with the Bradleys. As Walter Bradley had not yet moved out, Rose slept with Ada in her bed.

Despite all the misgivings, the arrangement seemed to work very well. Every morning Rose would accompany Ada on her journey to work and she even managed to acquire a job for herself, but the situation started to deteriorate when, for unknown reasons, Rose was fired from her job in August 1922. This, of course, meant that she was again penniless but the kindly Bradley's did not throw her out of their home, but allowed her to continue to live with them.

Life ticked on as normal until Walter's Christmas leave in 1922, which he spent with the Bradleys. He and Ada became engaged and planned that they would marry on the 2nd of June 1923. This sparked a very bad reaction in Rose, who displayed obvious signs of jealousy but she wasn't jealous because Walter wanted to marry Ada and not her; she was extremely jealous that Ada allegedly loved someone other than her. It was speculated that Rose was madly in love with Ada, that she and Ada had shared a bed during the whole time that Rose lived with the Bradleys and that the pair enjoyed a lesbian relationship. Rose did everything that she possibly could do to cause trouble between Ada and Walter including telling people that Walter had a venereal disease and that the couple had been found in bed together ... .a big scandal for "respectable" people in the 1920s of course.

It is possible that the reason for Rose's behaviour was jealousy but I think that it is more likely that it was fear. After the wedding, Ada would be living at the Barracks in London with Walter and that would leave Rose friendless, homeless and destitute again. She had no job and no income. Had her behaviour been different maybe the Bradleys would have allowed her to continue in their home as a lodger so long as she found a job and could pay them rent for a room, but her behaviour was so impossible that the Bradleys had reached the end of their tether with her and on Saturday the 31st of March Mr Bradley gave her an eviction order to be out of the house by Saturday the 14th of April.

Walter came home on leave on the 1st of April for the Easter holiday and doing their best to ignore Rose and her trouble making the family chatted excitedly about the upcoming wedding which was only two months away. Plans for the wedding were being discussed. Ada had just had the fitting for her wedding dress and Walter had had his leave of absence approved. What they did not know was that Rose had a terrible plan of her own which she would soon put into action.

In spite of all the trouble between them, Rose had continued to accompany Ada on her walk to work every day. Seeing as Rose was on notice of eviction and obviously angry and resentful this was probably not at all a sensible idea. A neighbour understood the potential danger that Ada was putting herself in and warned Mr Bradley about it, advising that he ought to accompany Ada to work himself but her warning was ignored. Ada was on the early shift on Wednesday the 11th of April and at 5.45 am that morning the pair set off for their walk down Langsett Avenue towards the Asylum, but Ada never got to work that morning. As they walked along, Rose suddenly pulled a hammer out from her coat and started hitting Ada over the head with it before taking out a razor and slashing her throat. The attack was sudden and unexpected and Ada had no chance to defend herself. Her screams alerted two nurses from the asylum who rushed out to try and help her. Rose screamed at them "I intend to kill her. I intend her to die. I will do you in too!". More people soon arrived at the scene including orderlies from the asylum who managed to take the hammer and razor from Rose and restrain her.

Someone stopped a passing motorcyclist and Ada was gently placed into his sidecar. The two nurses got into the sidecar with her, and the driver set off to take her up into the asylum but it was too late for Ada. There was nothing that medical staff could do to help her because the attack had killed her.

Walter was given the terrible news at the barracks in London. His beautiful fiancee was dead; murdered by the woman who had given her a home and friendship. The wedding that they had been happily planning a few days earlier would never take place. One can only imagine how devastating that news must have been for him.

Rose was bundled into a passing tram and taken to the police station and arrested on suspicion of murder. She was taken to The Central Police Court later that day and charged that "you did feloniously, wilfully, and of malice aforethought kill and murder Ada Bradley". She was remanded in custody for a week.

The inquest into Ada's death took place the next day, Thursday the 12th of April. When she was arrested Rose had handed in a letter that she had written to Mr Bradley on the afternoon of Saturday the 8th of April. This was read out at the inquest and The Sheffield Independent newspaper printed the details of the letter the next day:

"Dear Mr Bradley,

I am sorry to bring this trouble to you after you have been so good to me, but I cannot see my way clear to have my revenge any other way on your Ada, Cooper, and your wife, as they are all three against me. You have heard their tales together, but it is, as I said to you on Saturday morning when you told me I must leave your house. I knew it was no good complaining against such a seat of liars. Your wife said she would make a bad enemy, but when she sees this she will see I have made a worse enemy. I am writing this letter in the back bedroom on Saturday afternoon. Cooper told Ada not to go out with me; little does he think she won't be able to go out with him.

In the 1920's, inquests were different from today in that there was a jury in the Coroner's court who listened to the evidence and gave a verdict. The Coroner directed the jury that the only matter that they had to consider was whether, in their opinion, Rose Artliff had wilfully murdered Ada Bradley. It didn't take them long to return with their verdict that Rose had indeed murdered Ada and Rose was committed to stand trial at the next West Riding Assizes in Leeds.

The trial began on Friday the 11th of May. Rose was charged with murder. If Rose was found guilty she would face the hangman because in the 1920's being found guilty of murder carried a mandatory death sentence. The jury found her guilty but insane and the judge ordered that she be detained indefinitely "at His Majesty's Pleasure". "Thank you very much", Rose replied "I was guilty but I was sane".

Ada was laid to rest on the 13th of April 1923. There was a great outpouring of grief for the young nurse, with thousands attending the funeral.

Walter Cooper married Emma Hedditch in Portsmouth in 1927. Rose spent the rest of her life in the high security psychiatric hospital at Broadmoor where she died in 1973.

Thousands of people turned out at the funeral of Ada
Bradley

Her fiance Colonel Walter Cooper

Ada Bradley

CHAPTER ELEVEN: New Years Day 1960.The East House Pub Murders

Friday the 1st of January 1960. The first day of a new year and the first day of a new decade. I feel sure that there must have been a lot of optimism in the air and hope for the future. The previous three decades had been grim. The depression of the 1930's, the terrible world war in the 1940's and coming to terms with the massive work that needed to be done in the 1950's to repair the damage done by the war. Hopefully the 1960's would herald a better and brighter period and they did. Soon London was swinging and England was the place to be.

Not everyone was sharing this spirit of hope and optimism however. One of the people who wasn't was 30 year old Mohamed Ismail. He was born in British Somaliland (now Somalia) and he had moved to England seeking a better life in 1952 at the age of twenty-two. Things started out well. He had worked as a nurse in Somalia and soon secured himself a job at the Sheffield Royal Infirmary before moving on to work in the Sheffield steelworks at a company called Firth Vickers. Jobs in the steelworks were plentiful at that time and yet he was now unemployed. In view of the events that would soon follow it's likely that his mental health had been failing and that his employers had felt the need to dismiss him from his job.

He was clearly very unhappy on that first day of the new decade. He had had enough of life and confided to a group of women that he chatted with that he wanted to commit suicide but that his religion forbade it. If he killed himself he would go to Hell. With reasoning that made sense to him in his distressed and disturbed mind he reasoned that there was a way to end his own life without having to commit suicide. If he committed a murder he knew that he would be executed by hanging. That way he would be dead without breaking the rules of his religion and he would go to heaven. On the late evening of that New Year's Day he decided to put his deadly plan into effect. He left his home on Spital Hill in Burngreave and walked the short distance down the hill to the local pub which was called The East House. He walked into the pub to find a happy friendly atmosphere. Like most pubs in those days this pub had a piano and the pianist was playing. Five young men, out for a happy evening together, were standing around the piano singing along to the music when Ismail walked in. He walked up to them, pulled a gun from his pocket and pointed it at them. Given the happy atmosphere in the pub and the fact that in England at that time mass shootings were very uncommon the five young men thought it was a joke and they played along with it, holding up their hands in a mock surrender. This was no joke though. Five shots rang out and the five young men fell to the floor. 21 year old Michael McFarlane was killed outright. 29 year old Thomas Owen and 32 year old Frederick Morris died shortly after being admitted to the Sheffield Infirmary. Kenneth Ellis was shot in the wrist and the bullet went straight through his arm and lodged in the wall behind him. Michael McFarlane's brother Donald was shot in the head; leaving him seriously disabled for the rest of his life.

Pandemonium set in amongst the terrified customers but Ismail had achieved his objective and quickly left the room and went and barricaded himself into the Gents' toilet which was outside in the yard. Two police officers were soon on the scene and went outside to try to apprehend Ismail. Police constables Gilbert Robertson and Dennis Hastings told him to put his gun under the door and come out of the toilet but Ismail ignored them. In what can only be described as the most outstanding bravery the officers kicked the door in, took the gun (which was still loaded) from Ismail and took him into custody. The officers were wearing only their tunics, they had no weapons except their truncheons and they had no radio. They were in a small confined space with a man who had just shot and killed three men and yet they didn't hesitate to do their duty. Surely they should have received the highest of honours but they did not. They would both be dead before their bravery was finally acknowledged; PC Robertson having passed away in 1987 and PC Hastings in 2004.

They were both awarded posthumous bravery awards at the June 2023 South Yorkshire Police awards ceremony. Presenting the awards to their families the Chief constable of South Yorkshire Police, Lauren Poultney said:

"PCs Gilbert Robertson and Denis Hastings served their community with the utmost bravery that night, thinking quickly and diffusing the situation. Police officers can receive all the training in the world but nothing will quite prepare you for a situation like this which required them to risk their own safety to remove a weapon from a volatile situation."

Ismail was committed for trial at the Sheffield Assizes on 25th February 1960 but considered unfit to plead and committed to be detained at the high security Broadmoor Psychiatric Hospital. He told doctors that he heard voices in his head telling him what to do and they diagnosed him with paranoid schizophrenia. One would have thought that such a diagnosis would require a long period of treatment but twenty two months later he was deemed fit for discharge and deported back to Somalia.

We probably would not have known what happened to him after that if a friend of his called Daria Mohamed had not contacted The Star newspaper in 1984. Mr Mohamed, who had also come to England from Somalia, still kept in touch with friends back in his homeland. They told him that shortly after Ismail returned to Somalia in 1962 he had taken a pot shot at a judge in court. The judge was unharmed but Ismail had received a prison sentence of a few years. Shortly after his release he bought a gun and went on the rampage, killing a number of people in a village and was shot dead by police. So it appears that he had finally achieved what he had set out to do and committed murder so that he could be killed by the authorities and end his painful life without committing suicide. Did he end up in heaven though? Who knows?

The East House pub which was on Spital Street, Burngreave

PC Gilbert Robertson and PC Dennis Hastings were not honoured for their bravery until June 2023; sixty years after

the murders and when both these brave men were deceased

Michael McFarlane , Thomas Owen , and Fred Morris
who were murdered in the East House pub on New Years
Day 1960

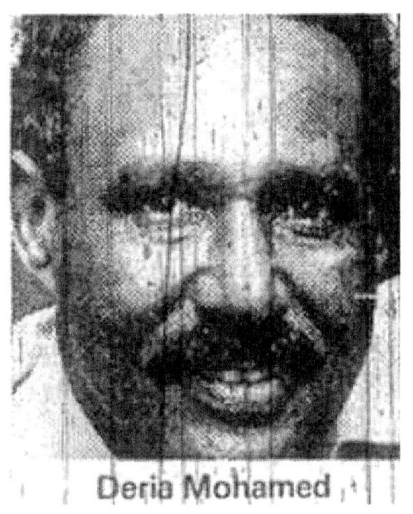

Deria Mohamed

Mohamed Ismail

CHAPTER TWELVE: Sheffield Gangs. The murder of William Plummer in 1925

Like many cities in England and the USA, Sheffield suffered intense gang activity in the 1920s, a period which was often referred to as the "Sheffield Gang Wars". The aftermath of The First World War left Sheffield grappling with many challenges. The steel industry which had boomed during the war faced a post-war slump which led to mass unemployment and financial hardship for many families. Much of the city's population lived in unsanitary overcrowded housing which was a breeding ground for disease. These factors led to the rise of gangs. For many young men, joining a gang provided a sense of belonging and a means of survival.

Initially the main gang in Sheffield was the Mooney Gang, led by George Mooney, which was based in the East End of Sheffield. The gang was involved in managing illegal gambling, in extortion and other illegal activities. During the First World War gambling had boomed, providing significant profits for the gang but the post-war economic slump which caused mass unemployment reduced people's disposable income meaning that they had less money available for gambling. As a result the gang's earnings began to decline and in order to maintain his own income he decided to dismiss most of the gang members, retaining only a very small number of his closest associates.

Unsurprisingly, the ones who were dismissed were not pleased and they decided to form a gang of their own. The new gang was called The Park Brigade and was led by Sam Garvin. The two gangs considered themselves above the law and the rivalry between them was intense. The gangs were very territorial and guarded their area with violence when necessary. The Park Brigade primarily controlled the Park district of Sheffield which included areas around Sky Edge. Sky Edge was a ridge of wasteland overlooking the Park district slums, and the gang operated an illegal gambling site known as the "Sky Edge Tossing Ring" there. The elevated position of the club was ideal as it made it easy for the gang to spot any approaching police officers.

(The Tossing ring game involved players tossing rings onto a target such as hooks or pegs to score points. The game, although simple, required precision and good hand-eye coordination. The players were highly competitive because there was illegal gambling on the outcomes.)

The Mooney Gang and the Park Brigade fiercely guarded their territories, maintaining their grip over the gambling rings and criminal activities but it was one chilling act of retaliation that ultimately unravelled the power of the Park Brigade leaders and exposed the brutal realities of gang violence.

The trouble started in a pub on an evening in April 1925 when Trimmer Walsh, one of the leaders of the Park Brigade got into an altercation with 27 year old William Plummer, an army veteran and former boxer, who was also drinking in the pub. Plummer intervened when he saw Walsh making unwanted advances towards a barmaid. Of course, the arrogant gangster Walsh wasn't taking that from anyone and a fight broke out between the two men but unfortunately for Walsh he was no match for a former boxer and Plummer gave him a good beating.

This was a public humiliation that the Park Brigade weren't going to ignore and a couple of days later on the 26th of April another two Park Brigade leaders - one of whom was 23 year old Wilfred Fowler - laid in wait to get the gang's revenge on William Plummer. Plummer was out with a friend of his called Jack Clay that evening and, like Plummer, Clay was also a former boxer. When they attacked, the two Park Brigade men soon found that they were no match for two powerfully built ex boxers and they were left bloodied and battered in the street. There was no way that this situation could be allowed to stand. The Park Brigade had now had three of their senior members beaten and defeated and their reputation had suffered major damage. They ruled the community by fear and they were also very much mindful of the fact that their great rivals The Mooney Gang would be thoroughly enjoying the situation.

If two gang members couldn't take down William Plummer then they needed to send a group of men that even he could not defeat. They acted quickly, and the next night a mob of about a dozen Park Brigade gangsters, led by 23 year old Wilfred Fowler and his 25 year old brother Lawrence, went to Plummer's home on Princess Street in Norfolk Bridge and shouted for him to come outside. The brave ex-soldier did just that and he was set upon by the mob and they kicked and stabbed him using knives, a chain and clubs. The police and emergency services were soon on the scene and he was taken to the Sheffield Royal Infirmary where he died from his injuries shortly after being admitted.

Unsurprisingly, onlookers were soon at the scene and the two brazen Fowler brothers sat on the steps of a nearby shop, claiming that they were only onlookers, but the police were having none of it and quickly rounded up the two brothers and five other gang members and took them to the West Bar police station. Sam Garvin was not so stupid as to sit around waiting for the police to arrive. He left the scene, caught a tram, travelled a short distance and got off and assaulted a man; thus creating an alibi for himself.

Thousands of people turned out at the funeral of William Plummer. A brave man who had fought for his country and who fell foul of murderous gang members for the "crime" of intervening to protect a barmaid.

The trial of the two Fowler brothers and five other gang members began at Leeds Assizes on the 28th of July 2025 with Mr Justice Finlay officiating. All were charged with the murder of William Plummer. The prosecution called fifty eyewitnesses and thirty expert witnesses. The two Fowler brothers claimed that they acted in self defence but this wasn't believed because there were so many witnesses to the attack who were giving their evidence. The bayonet which caused the injury that proved fatal was never found but witnesses testified that Wilfred Fowler had wielded it during the attack, while Lawrence had battered William with a truncheon. The jury found the two Fowler brothers guilty of William Plummer's murder and sentenced them to hang. Gang members George Willis, Amos Stewart and Stanley Harker were all found guilty of manslaughter, with Willis and Stewart being sent to prison for ten years, and Harker for seven years. Gang member Frederick Goddard was found not guilty and received no sentence. Despite extensive research, I've been unable to find out why Goddard was found not guilty. Sam Garvin was also found not guilty but he was given a sentence of twenty months for the assault he committed to create an alibi for the time of the murder.

The Fowler brothers appealed their conviction and the appeal was heard and dismissed at the Central Court of Criminal Appeal in London on the 18th of April 1926.

Wilfred Fowler was hanged at Armley Prison on the 3rd of September 1926 and Lawrence Fowler was hanged the following day.

It is surmised that the initial plan was for the two brothers to be hanged on the same day; the 3rd of September, as the hangman had been booked for two executions that day. The wardens, however, fearing that there might be trouble between the two brothers felt it would be better and safer to hang them on separate days and so a 25 y three year old man called Alfred Bostock was hanged on the same day as Wilfred Fowler.

The horrific murder of a brave young man who had fought for his country was the final straw for the Chief Constable of Sheffield, Colonel John Hall-Dalwood and four days after the murder he formed The Special Duty Squad, which later became known as The Flying Squad. Their sole mission was to break the gangs and they set about it with vigour although their heavy handed methods would not be deemed acceptable nowadays. The Squad conducted frequent raids on gambling dens and hideouts; sometimes using excessive force. Arrested gang members were often paraded through the streets to publicly humiliate them and undermine their reputation and their influence. In some cases the families of arrested gang members would also be subject to police pressure and scrutiny. The Chief Constable's methods were effective in curbing gang violence but they raised ethical concerns which eventually led to his resignation in 1926.

His successor as Chief Constable was Captain Percy Sillitoe who became famous as the "Gang Breaker". His methods of breaking the gangs obviously did not harm his career because by the time he retired he was the Director of MI5. He described his methods in his autobiography "Cloak Without a Dagger". He said "There is only one way to deal with the gangster mentality. You must show that you are not afraid. If you stand up to them and they realise you mean business they will knuckle under. The element of beast in man whether it comes from an unhappy and impoverished background or from his own undisciplined lustful appetites, will respond exactly as a wild beast of the jungle responds - to nothing but greater force and greater firmness of purpose". He was obviously a very successful person and I will leave him here with those last words on the subject.

I was curious though about the circumstances that had brought Alfred David Bostock to the gallows. Strictly speaking, it isn't a Sheffield crime because it happened in Rotherham, a town which adjoins Sheffield. It was a story as old as time; a married man having an affair with another woman. Twenty five year old Bostock was a crane driver at the Iron Works in Parkgate, Rotherham and twenty four year old Elizabeth Sherratt worked there in the offices. Bostock told her that he was very unhappy in his marriage and, despite the fact that he had a very young son, he was intending to divorce his wife. In order to keep the affair secret, Elizabeth left her job at the Iron Works and started working as an usherette at a cinema.

Before long the inevitable happened. Elizabeth got pregnant; but still believing that he was in the process of getting a divorce the relationship continued. However, eight months into the pregnancy, with Bostock still married and living with his wife and son, she started to have doubts about his intentions and about her own future and she told Bostock that she would be taking him to court for maintenance of the child. That caused Bostock to panic and, in his worried state, he foolishly talked to a couple of his workmates. A friend called Cecil Day told him that he was planning to go out to Sheffield with a group of friends, hoping that they would be able to pick up some girls there. Bostock told him not to go as he would only get himself into the same trouble that he was in. When Cecil asked him what trouble he was in he said that he had got a girl into trouble and that she was planning to take him to court for maintenance and that if she did he would have to "do her in".

Cecil said to him "Don't be so daft". The other workmate that he confided in was a man called Edwin Hurst. He told him that he was married and that he had got a girl into trouble and that if she persisted in her threat to take him to court for maintenance he would have to do her in. A few days later Edwin said to him "Has it come off yet?". Bostock replied "No. I have not seen her yet. I'm going to send her a letter to meet me but if everything doesn't go alright I shall do her in". Neither of these men went to the police to inform them about what Bostock had said, but that's not really surprising. I expect they thought that it was just bravado and that he wouldn't actually "do her in".

These were no idle threats however and on the evening of Sunday the 3rd of May 1925 he met Elizabeth in Parkgate and she did not return home that night. She lived with her parents and they reported her missing. A search was organised but they could find no trace of Elizabeth. Her badly beaten body was found in the river the next day. Although they strongly disapproved of her affair with Bostock, they were aware of it and so they told the police about it. They said that Elizabeth had gone out with the intention of meeting Bostock the previous evening. This, of course, made him the obvious murder suspect and when the family produced a letter from him arranging to meet her he was arrested and charged. The letter read:

"Dear Lizzie.

Could you possibly see me at the bottom of Green Lane on Sunday night at 7 o'clock. I want to see you, so don't forget. If you can't come, drop a line to the Parkgate Iron and Steel Company, Parkgate. That will find me, but I would like to see you.

So long, Alf.

PS Bring this letter and any other of my letters with you. I have something to show you. I shall come up the field way."

His trial began on the 27th of July 1925 and the evidence against him was overwhelming. The post mortem examination had shown that there was no water in Elizabeth's lungs, which ruled out drowning and she also had massive injuries to her head. Many witnesses came forward with evidence which it was really impossible to dispute. It took the jury only two hours to return their verdict of "Guilty" and the judge delivered the sentence of death.

An appeal was lodged in August but the Lord Chief Justice who heard the case stated that he felt that there was plenty of evidence from witnesses who saw the couple together on the night of her death. Combined with that were the remarks that the prisoner had made about "doing her in" and then the woman was found murdered. He said that his letter telling her to give His Lordship dismissed the appeal, stating that there was nothing in the appeal to change his mind. As we know, he was hanged at Armley Prison on the 3rd of September 1926.

CHAPTER THIRTEEN: Murder in Dore 1983. "The Fox". Arthur Hutchinson

Most of the crimes written about so far have taken place in the poorer working-class areas of the city but the more affluent, middle class areas have also suffered from horrendous crimes. One such crime was committed in Dore, which is reputedly Sheffield's wealthiest suburb. The date was 23rd October 1983.

The previous day had been planned so meticulously and happily by 59 year old solicitor Basil Laitner and his 53 year old wife Dr. Avril Laitner - the wedding of their elder daughter Suzanne. After a beautiful white wedding 250 friends and relatives gathered at the Laitners' home for a lavish reception. A very large marquee had been erected in the garden and the champagne flowed, the buffet was exquisite and a very good time was had by all. Whilst the reception was still in full swing the bride and groom were waved off to start their honeymoon and the guests continued the celebrations.

Eventually, as the evening wore on, the party started to wind down with guests thanking the Laitners for a wonderful day and setting off for home. As midnight approached, the Laitners - Basil, Avril, their 28 year old son Richard and 18 year old daughter Nicola all went wearily to bed. I'm sure that they were very pleased with how the day had gone and did only a minimum of clearing away. Tomorrow would be soon enough to attend to all that. What Basil, Avril and Richard could not possibly have imagined in their worst nightmare was that for them, there would be no tomorrow because an horrific tragedy was about to unfold.

Exactly a month earlier, on 23rd September 1983, a man called Arthur Hutchinson had escaped from the Magistrates' court in Selby North Yorkshire and gone on the run. He had pretended that he needed to go to the toilet and he was released from his handcuffs. He made his way upstairs and threw himself through a plate glass window. He cut his wrist and landed in a barbed wire fence, injuring his leg. He was wounded but he was free and now on the run; a fugitive from justice. He was a very dangerous individual with a long history of violence; committing rapes, thefts and burglaries and had very recently finished his latest five year prison sentence and been released. That sentence had been imposed because he had twice tried to shoot and murder his half-brother Dino Reardon. After his escape from the Magistrates' Court Dino and his wife had been given 24 hour protection by the police as it was feared that he would go and finish what he had started and that he would hope to be successful at his third attempt at murdering Dino.

However, Hutchinson was not in Selby in late October, he was forty-five miles away in Dore in Sheffield. Why that would be the case is not clear as there is no evidence of a connection to the city. He had been on the run for a month by then; he was filthy and in pain from the wounds that he incurred when he escaped from the Magistrates' court. I would guess that he had been lurking near the Laitners' house, saw the marquee and waited for his chance to go inside the marquee where there was probably food and alcohol that he could enjoy after the guests had all gone. If he had eaten and drank and then gone on his way there would have been no great harm done but this man was a thief and a burglar, and even more worryingly he was also a rapist and a man who had tried to murder his brother. Maybe he had been watching and had seen 18 year old Nicola go inside the house with her brother and her parents after all the guests had gone and she was a temptation he couldn't resist. He didn't enter the house straight away because he didn't want to confront four adults who could probably overpower him. He waited until all the lights went out in the house and made his move; entering the house quietly through a faulty patio door.

Obviously he didn't know which bedroom Nicola would be in. Maybe if he had got to her bedroom first he might have raped her and left, but the didn't. The first bedroom that he came to was Richard's and Hutchinson stabbed him repeatedly in the chest and neck. Basil Laitner heard the commotion and rushed to see what was happening. He didn't make it as far as Richard's bedroom because Hutchinson met him on the landing and stabbed him three times, causing him to fall down the stairs, fatally injured. Avril slept in a downstairs bedroom and he knew he had to get rid of her if he wanted to get to the object of his desire; 18 year old Nicola. No doubt Avril had heard the cries and struggles of her husband and son, and was terrified but ready to do her best to defend herself. She put up a brave struggle but she was no match for a vicious killer with a knife. He stabbed her twenty-six times leaving her dead on the floor. Having murdered all the people in the house who might have been able to defend her, he turned his attention to the object of his affections, Nicola Laitner, and set off upstairs to find her.

One cannot even begin to imagine how terrified Nicola must have been. Hutchinson walked into her bedroom and shone a torch into her eyes so that she couldn't see. Then he raped her at knifepoint before making her get out of bed and walk downstairs with him, causing her to have to walk through the blood of her father who was lying dead at the bottom of the stairs, and then through the patio door and out into the marquee. Once there he blindfolded and handcuffed her and raped her again. Then he set about eating and drinking from the leftover buffet food as he bragged about his crimes and about how he was nicknamed "The Fox" due to his ability to hide and outwit the police. They would never catch him, he told her. The only person who called him The Fox was himself with his grandiose and unjustified sense of how very clever he was.

Having eaten and drunk his fill, he marched Nicola back upstairs and raped her for the third time. For reasons known only to himself he did not kill her. He bound her hand and foot and left the terrified traumatised girl in that house of horror.

Two workmen who came to the house the next day to dismantle the marquee were the ones to discover the tragedy and they quickly contacted the police. Nicola was too traumatised to be able to say anything for several days. She was made of stern stuff however, and no doubt very keen to see the monster who had murdered her parents and brother taken off the streets to prevent him going on to murder anyone else. As soon as she was able she gave the police a detailed description of Hutchinson, from which an artist drew a likeness. This was made public and an officer from North Yorkshire police informed Sheffield police that the likeness looked like their suspect Arthur Hutchinson who was on the run. The media then published a photo of Arthur Hutchinson asking people to provide any information that would help the police to apprehend him before he was able to strike again.

Nicola also informed the police that whilst in the marquee Hutchinson had eaten a piece of cheese and drunk champagne and this enabled detectives to gather important forensic evidence. They also managed to get a sample of his blood which came from a cut on his own hand which he suffered when Avril was struggling to defend herself as she was attacked.

Hutchinson's mother Louise Reardon appealed in the press for him to give himself up. Speaking to the Hartlepool Mail newspaper on the 31st of October, she said:

"Arthur has always been such a good boy. He always remembers his mother. Just before he left for the last time he brought me a big bunch of flowers. He was the best lad I ever had. He used to do everything for me, the shopping, the washing,, the gardening. The only thing he wouldn't do was take me out in my wheelchair." She also said that he had posted her a birthday card after his escape from Selby Magistrates' Court and before the murders in Sheffield.

I can well understand a mother's love for her son, but to describe him in such glowing terms after his string of terrible crimes, especially after attempting twice to murder her other son Dino Reardon, is hard to believe. One has to wonder how Dino, a hard working respectable married man, felt to hear her describe Hutchinson as "the best lad she ever had".

His mother's words provided the police with a major lead however. They guessed that it was highly likely that he would try to get to his mother's house and they tapped her phone. They weren't wrong and they overheard him telling her in a call that he would be home to see her soon. All their resources were centred around the area where she lived and there was a 24 hour watch on her home.

Their suspicions proved to be right. After stealing and abandoning two cars to get to his home town of Hartlepool he called his mother at 4 am on the 4th of November and told her that he was coming home. The call was traced to a nearby phone box and four hundred police, police dogs, and mounted police searched for him with a helicopter overhead assisting in the search. Early on the morning of 5th November he was spotted in a field, brought down by a police dog and placed under arrest.

His trial began on the 11th of September 1984. He was accused of the three murders and the rape and pleaded "Not Guilty". The trial lasted only three days and it took the jury only four hours to find him guilty on all four counts and on the 14th of September he was sentenced to life imprisonment with a recommended minimum term of eighteen years. With such a sentence he could potentially be a free man at the age of only 60 in 2002. He was incarcerated in Wakefield Prison where prison warders described him as being like a ticking time bomb about to blow its fuse.

Leon Brittan, the Home Secretary at the time, did not agree at all with the possibility that he might be freed in 2002 and changed the sentence to a whole life term, meaning that Hutchinson would die in prison. He was still in prison in 2008 when, on the 16th of May, an appeal was heard by the High Court. His solicitor contended that the whole life tariff breached his human rights, but the Judge Mr Justice Tugendhat ruled that Hutchinson must never be set free and that the whole life tariff must stand.

Not satisfied with this ruling his solicitor referred his appeal to the High Court again on the 6th of October 2008 but the three judges hearing the case said that the crimes that he had committed were the worst that they had ever had to deal with and rejected his appeal and said that the whole life tariff must stand.

On the 1st of June 2015 his case was referred to the European Court of Human Rights (ECHR) claiming under Article 3 that his whole life sentence amounted to "inhuman and degrading treatment" because he had no hope of release. The Grand Chamber of the ECHR heard the case on the 21st of October 2015 but they denied his appeal and the whole life tariff was once again confirmed.

His case was heard again by the ECHR on the 17th of January 2017.but once again he was unsuccessful and his whole life tariff sentence was confirmed. The ECHR said that the United Kingdom had the right to impose whole life orders in appropriate circumstances.

I have the utmost sympathy for Hutchinson's mother and for his half-brother Dino Reardon (they shared the same mother but had different fathers, and were not brought up together). From everything that I have read they were completely respectable people but I do find some of what they said about Hutchinson extremely puzzling. His mother said that he had "always been a good boy". This was the man who had a long history of crimes including burglary, theft, sexual violence and rape. It also included being imprisoned after two failed attempts to murder her other son Dino. I understand the love of a mother, but I really do not understand this. In terms of saying that Hutchinson was "the best lad she ever had"; this must have been very hurtful and like a punch in the stomach to her son Dino.

However, I also find his feelings about Hutchinson very puzzling. Speaking to the Craven Herald and Pioneer newspaper in 2015 after the ECHR turned down his appeal he said that, despite the fact that he and his wife had been put under twenty-four hour protection whilst Hutchinson was on the run, he believed that his brother was innocent of his crimes against the Laitner family. He told the newspaper reporter:

"I am disappointed. I didn't think it was a fair trial. His sentence should never have been increased. He did some bad things in his time, and he certainly tried to kill me twice, but I don't think he carried out the murders. I don't like the bloke but I do believe that when someone has been sentenced and they do their time that should be it. I don't think anybody should be able to change that original sentence. If you're sentenced to a given number of years that should be it".

He says that "he certainly tried to kill me twice" but yet he does not think that he committed the murders of the Laitner family despite the fact that Nicola was in the house when the atrocities were committed and subjected to the most appalling crime herself. She knows with absolute certainty that it was Hutchinson who murdered her parents and her brother. I find it completely incomprehensible how he could survive two murder attempts by Hutchinson, ignore what was virtually an eye-witness account by Nicola and think that Hutchinson did not commit the crimes against the Laitners.

Unfortunately, I haven't been able to find any details about why Hutchinson tried to murder Dino or why the two attempts to shoot and kill him were unsuccessful. If anyone has any information that they would like to share I would love to hear from them: rjhensby@yahoo.com

Arthur Hutchinson remains in prison. He will be 84 years old in February 2025.

My last thoughts have to be about the Laitners. If anyone was ever subjected to "inhuman and degrading treatment" it was this family. It is inhumanity that is beyond belief. Suzanne and Nicola Laitner and their families moved to a different part of the country and changed their identities to try to shield themselves from all the publicity surrounding Hutchinson's endless appeals.

Avril Laitner and Basil Laitner posing happily at their daughter's wedding

Their son Richard Laitner who was also murdered by Arthur Hutchinson that day

Arthur "The Fox" Hutchinson

CHAPTER FOURTEEN: The Ughill Hall Murders in 1986

Ughill is a small village about five miles north-west of Sheffield City Centre in the parish of Bradfield. It is surrounded by rolling hills and lush green countryside. Within the village was a beautiful 18 room mansion called Ughill Hall and in April 1986 a Sheffield Solicitor called Ian Wood rented the property so that he could move in with his French lover Danielle Lloyd and her two young children; five year old Christopher and three year old Stephanie.

Wood had left his wife Margaret and their three children and 38 year old Danielle Lloyd was in the process of divorcing her second husband Colin Lloyd - the father of her two young children when the pair moved into Ughill Hall together in April 1986 and French-born Danielle reverted to calling herself by her maiden name which was Ledez.

Wood had been born into a wealthy family and privately educated. His father was director of a family company called John Wood and Son which specialised in ship repairing, marine engineering and fishing operations. Despite all the apparent success o f this family, tragedy had struck in 1984 when Wood's father committed suicide by shooting himself.

At the age of thirty-seven Ian Wood was a very successful man by anybody's measure. A qualified solicitor, he had founded his own legal practice in Sheffield and   was secretary of the local branch of The Law Society. Now he had a mansion to "advertise" his success and he and Danielle threw lavish parties to which the great and the good in Sheffield were invited.

For whatever reasons this apparently Utopian existence lasted only five months before shots rang out at the Hall leaving Danielle and Stephanie dead, Christopher seriously wounded with life-changing injuries, and Ian Wood on the run.

One can only speculate as to why Wood would shoot his lover and her two young children. Maybe he had a genetic mental flaw. In 1985 his doctor had raised concerns with the authorities about the fact that he had a gun licence. He was concerned about Wood's mental health and alcohol problems, bearing in mind that his father had committed suicide by shooting himself a year earlier in 1984. His gun licence was very temporarily removed, but soon returned to him. Ominously, the gun that shot Danielle and her children was the same gun that his father had used on himself to commit suicide.

Why would Wood want to murder Danielle? Maybe it was because at the time of her death Danielle was ten weeks pregnant and Wood did not want to become a father again. It was discovered after the murders that he was having an affair with another woman and maybe his plan was to get rid of Danielle,her unborn child and her two children and start again with this woman. I am completely puzzled about why he needed to murder Danielle and the children. They had not lived together for long and he could have told her that he didn't think that things were working out and that she should leave. He could easily have rented a small house for her and the children to move into - maybe paying the rent for a few weeks until she could get welfare benefits sorted out.

The unborn child would be her problem not his and he could always tell his friends and associates that he did not believe that the unborn child was his. It was also highly likely that Danielle's husband Colin Lloyd would have taken her back, especially since that would mean his two young children returning to him. Maybe a psychiatrist could make sense of this but I really cannot.

Whatever the reason, he clearly wanted to be rid of Danielle and her two children and at midnight on Sunday the 21st of September 1986 he took the necessary action to make it happen. In what he later described as a suicide plot between Danielle and himself they made love for the last time before he shot her in the back of the head; killing her instantly. No doubt at midnight the two children would be asleep in bed but the noise of the gunshot would probably have woken them. He went into Stephanie's bedroom and shot her. Her eyes remained open and so he shot her again to make sure that she was dead. There are differing accounts as to where Christopher was when he was shot. One report says that he was in the bathroom. Wherever he was, I'm sure that having heard all the gunshots he was trying to hide himself. Wood found him and, as he had done with Stephanie, he shot the child twice but even that didn't kill the poor boy. He was still groaning so Wood took a heavy metal ruler and battered him about the head with it.

According to media reports he packed his bag, left the gun in the kitchen and rang the police before fleeing the scene with £200.000 stolen from clients' accounts. On the evening of the next day Wood rang the police and they rushed to the house which was securely locked. They broke in and came upon the dreadful scene; two dead bodies and a seriously wounded child. Despite the cruel merciless attack on Christopher he had not died and he had been left lying alone in that house of horror for twenty-one hours before the police went to the house and found him. He was transferred immediately to the Sheffield Children's Hospital and survived but with life changing injuries.

A manhunt was now on. The registration number of the car that he had fled in was given out to the public but they were warned not to approach him and 24 hour police protection was provided to the Wood and Lloyd family homes.

Wood made repeated calls to a reporter at The Sheffield Weekly Gazette, saying that he wanted to give his side of the story, but he would not tell her where he was. During some of these calls he seemed to be suicidal. On Thursday the 25th of September a receptionist at the AA office in Barnstaple informed the police that a man answering Wood's description had requested an international driving licence and Interpol were informed of this. The search for Wood was focussed on France from that point onwards, especially around Amien where Danielle had been born and raised. Their hunch that Wood might have travelled to Amien proved to be correct because that was where, on Monday the 29th of September he was finally found.

He had joined a party of tourists doing a tour of Amiens Cathedral. He sneaked away from the group and climbed over a parapet and clung onto a gargoyle on the outside of the building. He was 200 feet from the ground and he was threatening to jump. A large crowd gathered around to watch what was happening, and whether he would jump. It took more than six hours for police officers and a priest to talk him down to safety and arrest him. He was extradited back to Britain and held in custody to await trial.

On the 1st of December 1986 he was charged with two counts of murder, one count of attempted murder and a charge of stealing clients' monies. His trial began in September 1987. He pleaded guilty to the murder of Stephanie, the attempted murder of Christopher and the theft of clients' monies but he did not plead guilty to Danielle's murder. He pleaded guilty to the manslaughter of Danielle, saying the he and she had agreed a suicide pact.

The Sheffield Star reported that:

"Under the terms of the pact, Wood had agreed that after killing Danielle and her children he was to visit a French church and light candles for her and her children; send a detailed explanation of the deaths to the press, kill Colin Lloyd, Danielle's husband; ensure that Danielle and her children were buried in a French village cemetery and visit their grave to lay flowers before taking his own life."

The prosecution did not accept his plea of a manslaughter charge and continued with the guilty charge. They argued that several of Danielle's French friends had been interviewed by the police and said that she had shown no signs of depression or of suicidal thoughts. Her mother had told investigators that she had spoken to her only hours before the murder and that she did not suspect that her daughter was at all suicidal.

To counter this, the defence called Ian Wood's mother, who said that Danielle had confided her suicidal intention to her on multiple occasions because she feared that her husband Colin would harm her or their son Christopher. She also said that her son Ian had called her less than twenty four hours before the shootings and explained the plan to her.

On the final day of the trial, the 30th of July 1987, the prosecution summed up by dismissing Wood's story of a suicide pact saying that he had killed Danielle out of obsessive hatred. The defence countered this by saying that he had nothing to gain by making up the suicide pact because he would be sentenced to life imprisonment for the murder and attempted murder of the two children anyway.

The jury agreed with the prosecution and the judge sentenced Wood to a life sentence for each of the two murders, twelve years for the attempted murder of Christopher and three years for the theft of client monies.

An appeal in 1989 was rejected and the sentences were upheld.
Having studied this case I do not believe that it is credible that Wood and Danielle entered into a suicide pact. Clever lawyer that he was I think that Wood was using this defence because The Homicide Act of 1957 states that if a person kills someone in pursuance of a suicide pact and then does not commit suicide themselves, they are guilty only of manslaughter and not murder.

This is a very puzzling case. I could not understand why Wood would need to murder Danielle and her children if he no longer wanted to be with her. All he had to do was tell her that the relationship was over and that she needed to leave Ughill Hall. Why didn't he just do that instead of murdering her.

Then I realised that the clue to the case is probably in the testimony given at trial by Wood's GP, Dr Alan Wales. He testified that, after a consultation on the 11th of November 1985 he advised the police that they should remove Wood's firearms licence due to his mental health and his alcoholism. The decision to report him to the police was supported by Wood's wife Margaret. Dr Wales told the court that Wood had appeared distressed and that he had prescribed antidepressant medication for him. The police did remove his licence but it was soon returned to him.

I realised that I had probably been working under a false assumption - an assumption that Wood planned and plotted to murder Danielle and the children. Having seen the evidence of Dr Watts I realised that this was most likely a wrong assumption. He had mental health problems and a serious alcohol problem. I think that on that September night he was unwell mentally and very very drunk. I think that Danielle and/or the children did something to annoy or upset him and in a drunken rage he shot Danielle, Suzanne and Christopher.

All murder cases are tragedies but it does seem that if Wood had received the psychiatric help he appears to have needed this one might have been avoided, instead of which his family, the Lloyd family, especially Christopher, and the Ledez family have to live with the ongoing ramifications of the crime.

To the best of my knowledge Wood continues to be incarcerated in Wakefield High Security Prison. He will be 76 years old this year (2025).

Ughill Hall where Ian Wood shot Danielle Lloyd and her two young children

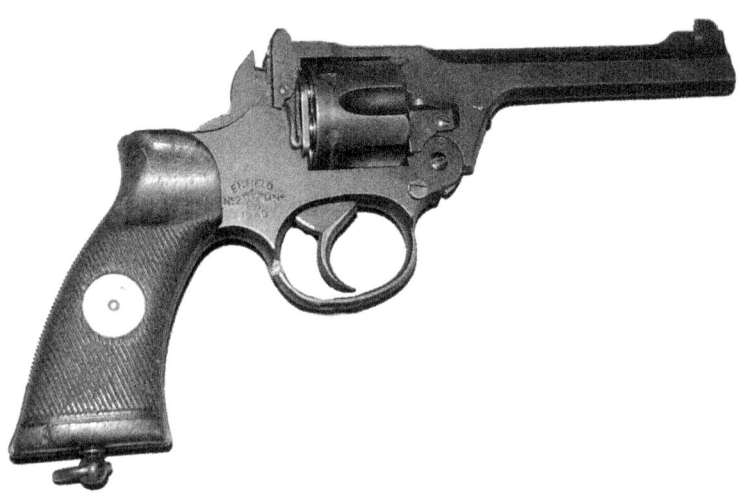

An example of an Enfield No.2 Mk I as used in the shooting

CHAPTER FIFTEEN: The murder of Dr Colin Shawcross in 1990

General Practitioner Dr Colin Shawcross and his wife Carol, who was also a GP, had a lifestyle that anyone could envy. They both worked hard at the profession they loved and were admired and respected by everyone that they came into contact with. By 2008 they had been married for 33 years, and they had raised three sons who were all doing well in life.

In late 2007, at the age of 56 and after thirty years of dedicated work at his surgery in Firth Park, Colin decided that the time had come to make life a little easier. He and his wife were already making tentative plans for what they expected to be a wonderful retirement together, and maybe Colin thought that to go suddenly from full time work as a doctor to complete retirement might be difficult so he decided to semi-retire instead. He resigned from his work as a GP and started to work part-time as a doctor at the Royal Hallamshire Hospital in Sheffield. I'm sure that his wife would have supported him wholeheartedly with that decision, but I'm also sure that in the coming years she must have regretted her support wholeheartedly.

His work at the Hallamshire was mostly in the Endoscopy unit and also working in the unit was a nurse called Julie Hill who was about ten years younger than him. They got on well and there was an obvious attraction between the pair and in January 2008 their relationship changed when they went from being friends to becoming lovers.

The affair continued secretly until August that year, and maybe if they had continued to keep it a secret it might have run its course and ended without any damage being done, but they didn't. They both decided that they wanted to end their marriages and start a new life together. It seems that Colin told his wife the news first, and he moved out of the family home and rented a small house in Aston close to where Julie, her husband Andrew and their twelve year old son lived. The house belonged to a couple who were neighbours and friends of Julie and Andrew and they had no idea that they had let the property to Julie's lover. Neither did Andrew Hill at that point.

I'm sure that Carol was devastated, but it seems that she took a mature approach to the situation and set about trying to "ride the storm" and do all she could to get her marriage back on track. Colin didn't remove most of his possessions from the family home and he was made welcome every time he visited his family home, which was often several times a week.

With her lover settled into his new home Julie broke the shattering news to her husband Andrew that she was in love with someone else and that she was planning to end their 15 year marriage and move in with her lover. Andrew did not take the news at all well. He was utterly devastated and told Julie that if she left he would commit suicide. She obviously took the threat seriously and decided not to leave.....for the time being.

Andrew decided that he would try to be the perfect husband so that his wife would change her mind and stay. He bought her things, spent money on home improvements and promised that he would buy her a sports car. He also rang Colin and implored him to finish the relationship and go back to his own wife. He probably pointed out that there was a twelve year old boy in this situation who would have his life torn apart if Julie left. He begged Colin to go back to his wife and end all contact with Julie.

However, the unhappy situation continued. Apart from the fact that their respective spouses and Colin's sons now knew about the affair, no-one else did. It continued in secret with Colin and Julie never going out socially together and Julie continuing to live with Andrew due to his continual threats to commit suicide if she left.

Colin spent the Christmas of 2008 back home with his wife and children and then things finally came to a head in January of 2009. Maybe Julie felt unhappy about Colin spending Christmas with his family or the fact that he seemed on friendly terms with his family and visited them regularly. Whatever the reason she decided to meet Colin and have it out with him. She said to Andrew that things couldn't go on as they were and that she was going to meet Colin to get the situation sorted out once and for all.

Andrew must have waited for her return with bated breath; hoping and praying that this would be the end of this long nightmare. She returned and told him that she and Colin had agreed that their affair was over for good. He was going to give up his rented house and return to his family and she would be staying with him and their son. One can easily imagine his relief.

It didn't last long though. When Julie's mobile phone bill arrived a couple of weeks later it showed that she and Colin had been ringing and texting each other regularly ever since she had told him that the affair was completely over. She had lied to him. Nothing had changed.

He confronted her on the 23rd of January and she told him that their marriage was over and she was moving in permanently with Colin. The docile, suicidal Andrew disappeared and he snapped. He had finally reached the end of his tether and flew into a terrible rage. As she tried to pack some clothes for herself and their son he snatched the clothes from her and threw them out of the window into the street. She tried to get away from him and leave with her son, but there was no way that he was going to let her take the car. She grappled with him and fell to the floor as he grabbed the keys from her hand. Then he picked up her mobile phone and completely smashed it up.

He was now completely out of control and his days of keeping everything quiet and private were over. He went round the houses of various neighbours to tell them that Julie had been having an affair with Dr Shawcross and that she was breaking up their marriage and leaving him. They couldn't believe it because they had known Julie and Andrew for years and had been friends as well as neighbours and had had no suspicion at all that something was badly wrong in the marriage.

One of the neighbours took Julie and her son in for the night and lent her a mobile phone. She texted Colin to tell him what had happened and he texted her back at 11.54 pm. She told him that she would come to his house at 7.30 the next morning. She did as she had promised but there was no sign of Colin. There was, however, a large pool of blood at the back of his house and she could see traces of blood on the driver's seat belt in Colin's Jaguar which was parked on the driveway. She dialled 999 and told the police what she had found, and told them about the horrendous row with her husband the previous evening.

The police immediately arrested Andrew. He didn't deny the problems with his marriage and the fact that his wife was leaving him to live with Colin but he denied any involvement in the apparent disappearance of Dr Shawcross and said that he had no idea where he was. Forensic experts examined the pool of blood and said that there was no way that anybody could have survived an attack of such ferocity without receiving urgent medical attention. Police contacted every hospital and GP surgery in the country to confirm that no-one matching Colin's description had been given medical attention. They also checked his bank accounts, mobile phone records etc to confirm that he was not still alive somewhere.

Despite the fact that there was no body, Andrew was immediately charged with murder and held in custody. They searched his house but found no bloodied clothes or shoes, but in those days most homes were heated with an open coal/coke fire so it is reasonable to assume that his clothes and shoes were quickly destroyed by burning them on the fire. There were, however, traces of blood in his wife's Honda Civic car. He was also seen with Colin's red Jaguar by a police dog-handler in the early hours of the morning after Colin's disappearance. He was sitting in the parked car on a remote track near to some fishing ponds not far from Colin's rented home. The officer went up to him and asked what he was doing. He said that the car was his and that he had stopped because it had run out of petrol. The officer had no reason at that point to think that the car driver had done anything wrong, but when he heard about the disappearance of Dr Shawcross the next day he realised the significance of seeing his red Jaguar and informed his superiors about it.

Hill said that he had no idea where Colin was and could barely remember what he looked like. He did come up with a suggestion about what might have happened though. He said that he had paid two Irish thugs £500 to put the frighteners on Colin; to threaten him and warn him to stay away from Julie. He said that he had never heard from them again and didn't know what they might have done. I think he must have been clutching at straws to come up with that one!

The days dragged on. Carol Shawcross and her three sons had to accept that something very bad must have happened to Colin and that he was never coming home. The situation must have been agony for them. Personally, I cannot think of a greater agony than that.

With her husband in custody Julie and her son returned to the family home. It wasn't until five months later that she realised that their wheelbarrow was missing and she immediately informed the police. Realising that it was possible that a wheelbarrow could have been used to transport a dead body they immediately set to work to find the wheelbarrow and hopefully Colin's body.

There is a 37 acre privately owned forest called Loscar Woods a 15 minute drive from Colin's rented home on Ashley Grove. Access is down a quiet B road. Was this the road where Andrew was spotted in Colin's red Jaguar in the early hours of the 24th of January? Police must have figured that if you were planning to bury a body without it being found a 37 acre wood would be an ideal place. They estimated that it would take at least two years to properly search such a large area, but luck was on their side. Not long after entering the wood, broken twigs and branches indicated that there had been some disturbance and they soon came upon a wheelbarrow and a spade. They dug around that area and found Colin's body buried in a five foot deep hole concealed by a tree stump.

Despite admitting that the wheelbarrow and spade were his, Andrew continued to deny any knowledge of the murder and stuck to his story about it being the work of the two Irish men that he had hired to "frighten Colin off" so that the affair would be ended and his marriage would be saved.

Having now found the body the police were satisfied that they had enough evidence to put Andrew Hill on trial for the murder of Dr Colin Shawcross and his trial began in January 2010.

The prosecution maintained that, after throwing his wife Julie out of the house, he drove to Colin's house in his wife's Civic Honda car. In a jealous rage he beat Colin over the head with a pick axe handle which fatally fractured his skull. He then dragged the body into Colin's jaguar and with the spade and wheelbarrow in the boot he drove to Loscar Woods and buried the body five feet underground. He then drove the Jaguar back to Colin's home, having been seen on that journey parked in the Jaguar by the police dog-handler. He then left the Jaguar at Colin's house and drove back to his own home in the Honda Civic. Evidence of blood being found in that car was also used against him.

On the 26th of January 2010 the jury found him Guilty of murder and, as Carol Shawcross gave a very moving account of how the loss of Colin had affected her sons and herself, Andrew clung to the security glass in front of him and wept. She said:

" It has brought indescribable distress and misery which has been compounded by the concealment of his body. Until his remains were found our lives were sad and our thoughts negative which adversely impacted on our professional, social and family life. Although we were temporarily separated we had discussed his return to the family home and I feel that given time we would have been reunited. His murder has robbed me of the companionship, contentment and security that Colin and I had planned in retirement".

The judge then sentenced him to life imprisonment with a minimum term of 17 years. He told Hill:

You have been found guilty of the murder of Dr. Colin Shawcross, a man who had devoted himself for 30 years as a GP to caring for the health and well being of his fellows. He still had a great deal to give both to society and his family. You acted in a devious, vengeful, cowardly and unmanly way. You deliberately armed yourself with a deadly weapon and engineered a situation where you were free to surprise Dr Shawcross and strike him."

When the judge described his story of hiring hard men as "utter fabrication" Hill shouted: "It wasn't sir".

As he was taken down to the cells he continued to protest his innocence. Six weeks after the trial he wrote to the Star newspaper saying:

" I have not killed anybody. I will never come to terms with having been found guilty of murder."

It is reported that he still maintains his innocence to this day. He will be eligible for parole in 2027. It has always been my understanding that a prisoner has to confess his guilt and show remorse before a parole board will agree to his release but that remains to be seen in this case.

Millions of people in this country and around the world cheat on their wife/husband/partner every day. Some are never found out and get away with it, some partners - usually wives - turn a blind eye, particularly if they have children and don't want the family to be broken up. In some cases the affair causes broken marriages and great pain for the "innocent" partner and particularly for children. However, an affair does not usually end in such a horrific way as this one did. A tragedy that wrecked two families.

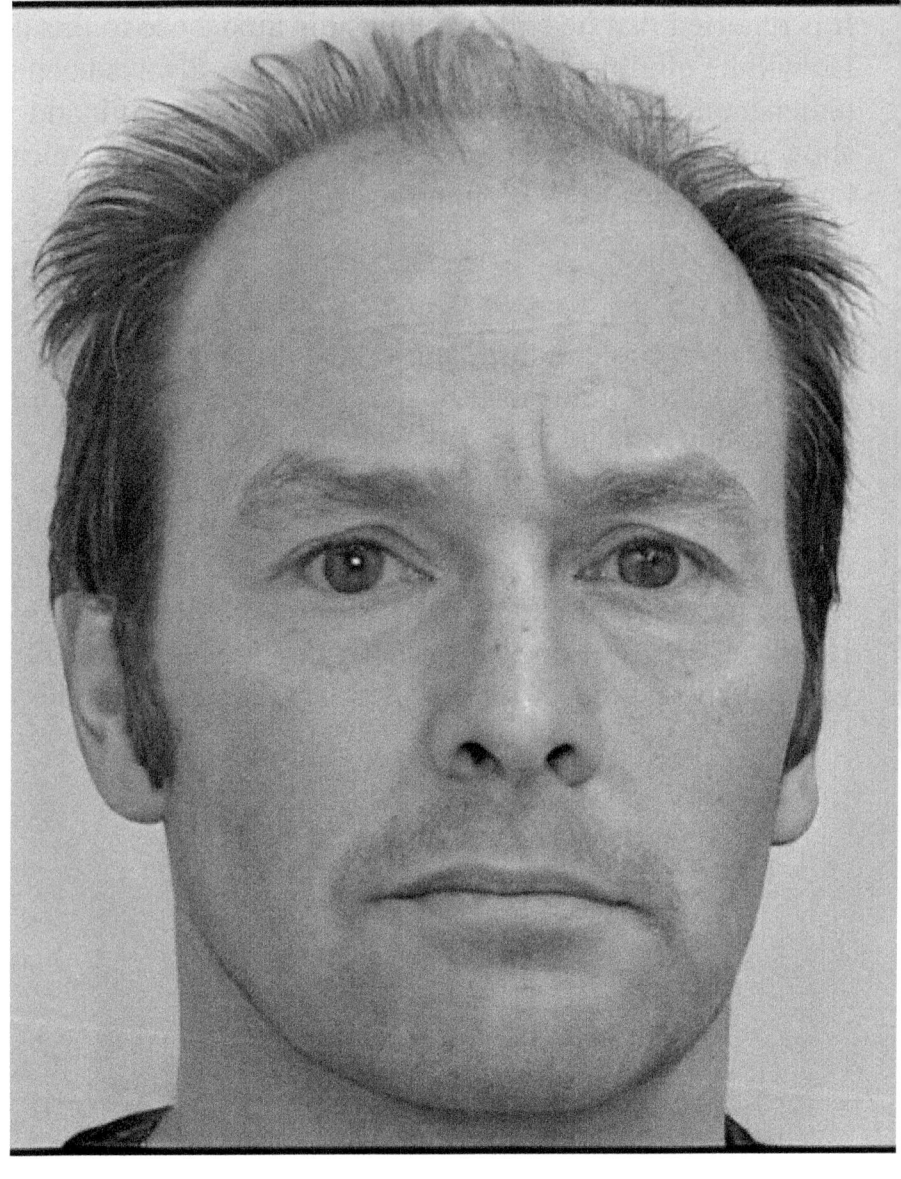

Andrew Hill, the jealous husband who murdered Dr Colin Shawcross

Dr Colin Shawcross whose body was not discovered until five months after he was murdered

If you found this book interesting. Please would you leave a review on Amazon?

You might find my book **"Was Elvis Murdered? and other true crimes from the dark side of Dixie"** of interest. In the following pages I give a brief synopsis of each of the crimes in the book. Each case is examined in full and in great detail.

Was Elvis Murdered?

I fell in love with Elvis when I was 7 years old and never fell out of love with him. I wrote this chapter of the book giving him the dignity and respect that this gentle, generous man deserves.

I remember the terrible news that spread quickly around the world on the 16th of August 1977: Elvis Presley, the King of Rock and Roll had died at the age of only 42. I remember being puzzled at the photograph of him in his coffin; it looked like Elvis when he was much younger, but still I believed that he was dead. Over the years it has become increasingly apparent that things were not as they seemed and in this chapter I examine five possible scenarios about what happened to him on that fateful day.:

1. He died of natural causes.

2. He committed suicide

3. He died from an accidental overdose of illicit or prescribed drugs.

4. He was murdered.

5. He might not have died at all.

Read all the evidence and see whether you agree with me about what really happened on the 16th of August 1977.

Justice Delayed is Justice Denied: George Stinney Jr.

In 1944 George Stinney Jr., a 14 year old African American boy, became the youngest person ever to be executed in the United States. He was convicted of murdering two young white girls In Alcolu, South Carolina. Despite the lack of any physical evidence and a rushed trial, a jury of 12 white men found him guilty. The terrified child was strapped into an electric chair that was too big for his small frame and executed. Read about this case and be horrified that such an inhuman thing could possibly be allowed to happen. It took a lot of work and 70 years before this terrible miscarriage of justice was finally overturned in 2024.

J.R. Hensby
The Boy They Electrocuted Twice: Willie Francis.

In 1946, Willie Francis, a 17 year old African American boy, survived a botched execution in Louisiana. As with George Stinney, this was another case of a young African American boy being found guilty of murdering a white person. On evidence that shouldn't have persuaded anyone of his guilt, the boy was found guilty of murdering a well-connected white man called Andrew Thomas. Aged only 16 Willie was sentenced to death. At the first attempt to execute him, the eclectic chair malfunctioned and he was taken back to prison to await a new date for the execution. This led to a year-long battle which eventually reached the U.S. Supreme Court. Despite the failed execution and the many questions surrounding his guilt he was executed successfully in 1947 at the age of 18. Whilst awaiting the second execution, he wrote a pamphlet describing the unique experience of sitting in the electric chair, expecting to die, as electricity shot into his body.

Last Words. The Execution of Stephen Michael West.

In 1986, Stephen Michael West, along with his accomplice Ronnie Martin committed the brutal murders of Wanda Romines and her 15 year old daughter Sheila Romines in their home in Union County, Tennessee. The victims were tortured and Sheila was raped before they were both stabbed to death. West was convicted of the murders and received the death penalty in 1987. Ronnie Martin was 17 years old at the time of the crime, and times had changed since George Stinney Jr. and Willie Francis had been executed at a young age. Under the law in 1987, Martin was too young to be executed and although he was arguably the more guilty of the two he was sentenced to life imprisonment. He remains in jail and will be eligible for parole in 2030. Despite being an exemplary prisoner whilst on death row West was executed in 2019; thirty three years after the murders.

Murder in Nashville: Janet Gail March.

In 1996, Janet Gail March, a children's book illustrator from Forest Hills, Tennessee, went missing under suspicious circumstances. Her husband, Perry March, claimed she left after an argument, but her car was found x, and evidence suggested foul play. Despite the absence of her body, Perry was later convicted of her murder in 2006, along with his father, Arthur March, who helped dispose of her body. Janet's remains have never been found. Unlike the previous three cases, the people involved in this terrible story were very well connected, high profile citizens of Nashville.

A Serial Killer? The Strange Case of Audrey Marie Hilley

Had someone written the story about Audrey as a work of fiction, it would have been laughed off as just too far - fetched and ridiculous. But it wasn't fiction, it was a true and completely unique story. She was certainly a murderer and possibly a serial killer. Her story seems unbelievable yet it is true and fascinating. Read it, and you'll see what I mean!

More Dead Husbands: Raynella Dossett Heath:

Raynella was accused of murdering two of her husbands: her first husband Ed Dossett, who was the Knox County District Attorney, in1992 and her second husband David Leath in 2003. Another fascinating case, with multiple trials and legal battles before finally having all charges dropped by a judge in 2017 due to insufficient evidence. Read it and see whether you think that the evidence was insufficient!

The Lover in the Closet: Martha Ann Freeman:

In 2005, Martha Ann Freeman was convicted of the murder of her loyal and loving husband, Jeffrey Freeman, in Brentwood, Tennessee. The case would probably not have gained a great deal of publicity except for the bizarre circumstances surrounding the crime. It gained a lot of notoriety when it appeared that Martha's lover, Rafael DeJesus Rocha-Perez had been secretly living in a closet in the couple's home for a month before the murder. Martha tried to pin the blame for the crime on her lover, but without success. Both were convicted of first degree murder and sentenced to life imprisonment.

J.R. Hensby

The Only Woman Ever Electrocuted in Georgia: Lena Baker:

Lena was an African American maid living in Cuthbert, Georgia. She worked as a maid for a man called Ernest Knight and in 1944 she was found guilty of murdering him. He had imprisoned her and threatened to kill her and during a struggle she shot him in self defence. She was executed by electrocution in 1945, becoming the only woman ever to be electrocuted in Georgia's electric chair. It took sixty years for the injustice of her trial to be acknowledged and she was posthumously pardoned in 2005.

The First White Woman Electrocuted in Alabama: Earle Dennison.

Of all the crimes that I have written about there is something exceptionally cruel about the murders committed by this woman. She was a trained nurse but in my opinion brought great shame on her profession even though it wasn't patients of hers that she murdered. Her victims were a young child and a newborn baby. Both were nieces of hers. The baby died of arsenic poisoning shortly after birth and her sister, two and a half year old Shirley Ann Weldon was poisoned a couple of years later. Shirley Ann was particularly fond of her Aunt Earle and when she visited on the 1st of May 1952 Shirley rushed to meet her and climbed on her knee for a cuddle. Aunt Earle had brought her an orange drink and Shirley sat happily on Earle's knee as she drank it. Before long she also died from arsenic poisoning. Wicked beyond belief. She was executed on the 4th of May 1953. What could possibly have been the motive for such evil?

Rev. John David Terry. The murder of James Matheny.

In the early 1980's the Rev. John David Terry was becoming
tired of being a church minister and he yearned for a new
life free of the burdens of ministering to his church flock,
and living with his wife and two sons. He didn't want to just
up and leave, he wanted a whole new identity and by 1987
he had made the necessary plans. He had stolen a significant
amount of church funds and got a driver's licence in the
name of a deceased baby boy called James Milsom. All he
had to do now was murder someone. He put his plan into
action on the 15th of June 1987. He lured his friend James
Matheney up into the attic of the church, shot him dead, and
set fire to the church. The authorities would find the charred
remains of a body, and assume that the Rev. John Terry had
been shot and killed in a robbery. He rode away from the
scene feeling full of joy. At the age of 42 he was free! The
Rev John David Tarry was no more and "Jerry Milsom"
rode off into the night to begin his new life. What could
possibly go wrong?

The Judge Who Overruled The Jury: The William Glen Boyd Case.

William Boyd and his accomplice Robert Milstead broke into the home of Fred and Evelyn Blackmon in Anniston Alabama in 1986. The men tied the couple up and lied to them by saying that they had kidnapped their daughter and needed a ransom to release her. Fred was accompanied to the bank to withdraw ransom money and The couple were then driven to a wooded area where they were shot to death. The motive seems to have been anger at Evelyn. Their daughter had had a relationship with Boyd but it had broken up and he believed that Evelyn felt that he was not good enough for her. This is another long and intriguing case. Eventually Milstead pleaded guilty and confessed to what had happened. Boyd went to trial and the jury found him guilty, but made a recommendation for mercy and a life sentence. The judge was having none of it and he ignored the jury and sentenced Boyd to death. He was executed by lethal injection on the 31st of March 2011.

Printed in Dunstable, United Kingdom

64272445R00088